PUFFIN BOOKS

Editor: Kaye Webb

FREAKY FRIDAY

'"Why don't you just let me be responsible for myself?"
I asked.

"You will be soon enough," mother said.

"Not soon enough to suit me," I snapped.

"We'll see about that," said mother.'

And then something astonishing happened. When Annabel woke up one morning she found she'd turned into her
mother! At least, she *looked* exactly like her but inside
she felt just the same. Well, what would you do in such
a situation? Annabel determined to enjoy herself, but
although remembering that your brother is your son and
your husband your father is rather fun, life gets more
complicated when the washing machine goes wrong, the
cleaning lady comes in drunk, and you realize you've forgotten to collect your son from school. And even worse
happens when you find out what that mysterious date in
your mother's diary means and you have to go to school
to talk about yourself! And, anyway, where *is* your
mother?

This is a hilarious story of an extraordinary day in the
life of ... mother? ... daughter? Sons and daughters of
ten and over will have a marvellous time reading it.

MARY RODGERS

FREAKY FRIDAY

PUFFIN BOOKS
in association with Hamish Hamilton Children's Books

Puffin Books, Penguin Books Ltd, Harmondsworth, Middlesex, England
Penguin Books, 625 Madison Avenue, New York, New York 10022, U.S.A.
Penguin Books Australia Ltd, Ringwood, Victoria, Australia
Penguin Books Canada Ltd, 2801 John Street, Markham, Ontario, Canada L3R 1B4
Penguin Books (N.Z.) Ltd, 182–190 Wairau Road, Auckland 10, New Zealand

—

First published in the U.S.A. 1972
First published in Great Britain by
Hamish Hamilton Children's Books 1973
Published in Puffin Books 1976
Reprinted 1977 (three times)

—

—

Made and printed in Great Britain by
Hazell Watson & Viney Ltd, Aylesbury, Bucks
Set in Linotype Pilgrim

For Nina, Kimmy, and Ma

One

You are not going to believe me, nobody in their right minds could *possibly* believe me, but it's true, really it is!

When I woke up this morning, I found I'd turned into my mother. There I was, in my mother's bed, with my feet reaching all the way to the bottom, and my father sleeping in the other bed. I had on my mother's nightgown, and a ring on my left hand, I mean her left hand, and lumps and pins all over my head.

'I think that must be the rollers,' I said to myself, 'and if I have my mother's hair, I probably have her face, too.'

I decided to take a look at myself in the bathroom mirror. After all, you don't turn into your mother every day of the week; maybe I was imagining it – or dreaming.

Well, I wasn't. What I saw in that mirror was absolutely my mother from top to toe, complete with no braces on the teeth. Now ordinarily, I don't bother to brush too often — it's a big nuisance with all those wires — but my mother's teeth looked like a fun job, and besides, if she was willing to do a terrific thing like turning her body over to me like that, the least I could do was take care of her teeth for *her*. Right? Right.

You see, I had reason to believe that she was responsible for this whole happening. Because last night, we had a sort of an argument about something and I told her one or two things that had been on my mind lately.

As a matter of fact, if it's OK with you, I think I'd better start back a little farther with some family history, or you won't know what I'm talking about or who (whom?).

My name is Annabel Andrews. (No middle name, I don't even have a nickname. I've been trying to get them to call me Bubbles at school, but it doesn't seem to catch on.) I'm thirteen; I have brown hair, brown eyes, and brown fingernails. (That's a joke — actually, I take a lot of baths.) I'm five feet; I don't remember what I weigh but I'm watching it, although my mother says it's ridiculous, and I'm not *completely* mature in my figure yet. Maybe by the summer though.

My father is William Waring Andrews; he's called Bill; he's thirty-eight; he has brown hair which is a little too short, but I've seen worse, and blue eyes; he's six feet (well, five eleven and a half); and he's a fantastically cool person. He's an account executive at Joffert and Jennings, and last year his main account was Fosphree. If you're into the environment thing at all, you know what that is: no phosphates, low sudsing action, and according to my mother, grey laundry. We had boxes of the stuff all over the kitchen. You couldn't *give* it away. This year, he has New Improved Fosphree (That's what they think!), plus something called Francie's Fortified Fish Fingers. *Barf* time! If there's anything more disgusting than fortified fish, I don't know what.

Oh yes, I do, I just thought of what's worse. My brother. He is I cannot begin to tell you how disgusting. It may not be a nice thing to say but, just between you and me, I *loathe* him. I'm not even going to bother to describe him – it's a waste of time. He looks like your average six-year-old with a few teeth out, except that, as my grandmother keeps saying, 'Wouldn't you know it'd be the boy who gets the long eyelashes and the curly locks? It just doesn't seem fair.' No, it certainly doesn't, but then what's fair? These days, not much. Which is exactly what I was trying to tell my mother last night when we had the fight. I'll get to that in a minute, but first a few facts about Ma.

Her name is Ellen Jean Benjamin Andrews, she's thirty-five – which makes her one of the youngest mothers in my class – she has brown hair and *brown* eyes. (We're studying Mendel. I must be a hybrid brown. With one blue- and one brown-eyed parent you're supposed to get two brown-eyed kids and two blue-eyed kids. So far there are only two kids in our family, but look who's already got stuck with the brown eyes. Me. The sister of the only blue-eyed ape in captivity. That's what I call him. The blue-eyed ape. Ape Face for short. His real name is Ben.) Anyway, back to my mother. Brown hair, brown eyes, and, as I've already mentioned, nice straight teeth which I did *not* inherit, good figure, clothes a little on the square side; all in all, though, she's prettier than most mothers. But *stricter*.

That's the thing. I can't stand how strict she is. Take food, for instance. Do you know what she makes me eat for breakfast? Cereal, orange juice, toast, an egg, milk, and two Vitamin Cs. She's going to turn me into a blimp. Then for lunch at school, you have one of two choices. You can bring your own bag lunch, with a jelly sandwich or a TV dinner (they're quite good cold) and a Coke, or if you're me, you have to eat the hot meal the school gives you, which is not hot and I wouldn't give it to a dog. Alpo is better. I know because our dog eats Alpo and I tried some once.

She's also very fussy about the way I keep my room. Her idea of neat isn't the same as mine, and besides, it's my room and I don't see why I can't keep it any way I want. She says it's so messy nobody can clean in there, but if that's true, how come it looks all right when I come home from school? When I asked her that last night, she just sighed.

A few other things we fight about are my hair – she wants me to have it trimmed but I'm not falling for that again (The last time it was 'trimmed' they hacked six inches off it!) – and my nails which I bite.

But the biggest thing we fight about is freedom, because I'm old enough to be given more than I'm getting. I'm not allowed to walk home through the park even with a friend, because 'New York is a very dangerous place and especially the park.' Everybody else's mother lets them, 'but I'm not everybody else's mother.' You're telling me!

Tomorrow one of my best friends in school who lives in the Village is having a boy-girl party and she won't let me go because the last time that friend had a party they played kissing games. I told her the mother was there the whole time, staying out of the way in the bedroom, of course, and she said, 'That's exactly what I mean.'

What kind of an answer is that? I don't get it. I don't get any of it. All I know is I can't eat what I want, wear what I want, keep my hair and my nails the way I want, keep my room the way I want or go where I want. So last night we really had it out.

'Listen!' I screamed at her. 'You are not letting me have any fun and I'm sick of it. You are always pushing me around and telling me what to do. How come nobody ever gets to tell you what to do, huh? Tell me that!'

She said, 'Annabel, when you're grown-up, people don't tell you what to do; you have to tell yourself, which is sometimes much more difficult.'

'Sounds like a picnic to me,' I said bitterly. 'You can tell yourself to go out to lunch with your friends, and watch television all day long, and eat marshmallows for breakfast and go to the movies at night . . .'

'And do the laundry and the shopping, and cook the food, and make things nice for Daddy and be responsible for Ben and you . . .'

'Why don't you just let me be responsible for myself?' I asked.

'You will be, soon enough,' she said.

'Not soon enough to suit me,' I snapped.

'Is that so!' she said. 'Well, we'll just see about that!' and she marched out of the room.

Two

ALL of which should explain why I wasn't as surprised as most people would be if they woke up in their mother's body.

I was a *little* surprised of course, but mostly I felt it was fantastically considerate of her. And imaginative. Instead of punishing me for rudeness, or crying phony tears like some mothers I know, she was just going to let me find out for myself. I could hardly wait. The whole day stretched out ahead of me. I was going to tell myself to do a whole bunch of fabulous things – as soon as the kids got off to school where – oh hey! oh wow! – I wasn't going to have to go! Not that I hate school. Actually, I like it, at least I like the people, but on the days when you haven't done all your assignments, Miss McGuirk (rhymes with work, shirk and *jerk*) gets mad, and this was going to be one of those days. I hadn't done any of it, not even the English composition I was supposed to hand in this week.

I flashed myself a radiant smile in the bathroom mirror and remembered that my first responsibility was to our teeth, which I brushed with great enthusiasm. Oh the smoothness of them all . . . a joy to the tongue! I rinsed and smiled again.

'Lovely. You're lovely. *I'm* lovely,' I thought. I took the rollers out, fixed my hair, put on a silky bathrobe, and looked myself over again. Even lovelier. But a bit pale, maybe?

The next twenty minutes I spent mucking around with the moisturizer and the foundation and the translucent powder and the TV Touch (That's wrinkle hider and I wonder why she bothers with it. We certainly don't need it.), the rouge, and the three different eye shadows, the eyelash curler and finally the mascara. How did I know what I was doing? You may well ask! I've watched her do it a hundred and one thousand times when she was going out on a festive occasion. It's easy.

'Oh my!' I whispered to the mirror. 'Aren't you something! Aren't you just something!'

Lately I'd been getting so fed up with my face and fed up with people saying how much I looked like my mother. My mother is always saying, 'Her father and I think Annabel looks like her very own self.'

You know why I think she says that? Because it's insulting to her to say I look like her. I guess I can't blame her. If I were Ma and had a daughter who looked like me, I wouldn't admit it either. Besides, I don't. Look like her, that is. I wish I did.

'Well, today I do, and it's a great improvement,' I thought to myself, and slinked out of the bathroom and into the bedroom where Daddy was still sleeping. I gave him a little punch on the shoulder to wake him up.

'Hey,' I said, 'are you awake?'

'I am now,' he said. 'Was I dreaming or did you just punch me?' I guess grown-ups don't punch each other awake. He looked sort of annoyed.

'You must have been dreaming,' I said. 'Anyway, now that you're up, how do I look?'

'What makes you think I'm up?' he asked, closing his eyes again and rolling over. 'I'm not at all up, I don't want to be up, and I don't know what *you're* doing up. As a matter of fact, what *are* you doing up? Is there something wrong?' He opened one eye.

'No, no, nothing,' I said in a hurry. 'I just wondered if you liked the way I look.' He opened the other eye, leaned on one elbow and blinked at me.

'Ellen, what is going on with you this morning?' (Ellen, he really thinks I'm Ellen. Isn't this the most marvellous, incredible . . .) 'Of course I like the way

16

you look. I always do. You look fine – a little fancy for this time of day, but fine.'

'You mean my face, Bill?' I asked.

'Yes, I mean your face; you don't usually put all that stuff on before breakfast, but you look great. You have a great face, I love it. I love you. OK? Now can I go back to sleep?'

Just then the alarm went off. Daddy groaned and I slinked off to the kitchen to make breakfast before he could say anything else. Somehow, I had the feeling that until he'd had some coffee, anything else he said wouldn't be too friendly. And then I realized that after he'd had the coffee he might not be too friendly either because he was going to get instant. It was the only kind I knew how to make.

Three

BREAKFAST went off not too badly, considering it was my first. Luckily, Daddy asked for fried (I learned how to do that a couple of years ago.) so I made fried, and toast. I also made a small mistake.

'Sorry about the instant, Daddy, but we're all out of regular,' I said, giving him a nice friendly kiss on the cheek.

'*Daddy!* Since when did you start calling me Daddy? You never did that before,' he said.

'No, and I won't again, Bill, dear,' I said, relieved at least that he wasn't going to make a scene about the coffee. I ran back into the kitchen to find out what Ape Face wanted.

'What'll it be for you, lover boy?' I asked, crossing my arms and giving him the hairy eyeball. Just watch him ask for scrambled!

'Could I have scrambled, Mommy, please?' What did I tell you!

'No, you can't,' I said, very briskly. 'I don't have time to wash two pans. It's fried or nothing.'

'But I don't like fried,' he said. (You know, she spoils him rotten, but not me!)

'Then eat cold cereal,' I said, slapping down a box of Sugar Coated Snappy Krackles in front of him.

'But these are Annabel's. She bought them with her own money to eat when she watches television. She'll kill me if I eat up her cereal,' he said anxiously. What a worrywart.

'Listen, Ben,' I said very slowly and carefully. 'Annabel *wants* you to eat her Sugar Coated Snappy Krackles. So eat 'em. NOW!' He jumped and started to eat.

Speaking of Annabel reminded me that I hadn't seen myself yet and she was going to be late for school if she didn't hurry. Me, she, I, her? I was getting very mixed up. I also wondered, as I stood outside the door to her room, what – who – I was going to find in there. Was it going to be Annabel's body with Annabel's mind in it, but I wouldn't know what the mind was thinking? Or was it going to be Annabel's body with Ma's mind in it, which would certainly be a more tidy arrangement?

Whoever-it-was was lying on her stomach on the bed, waving her feet in the air and reading a comic book. It certainly looked like Annabel. It looked like her room, too. There were all kinds of clothes dribbling out of drawers and hanging around on the floor. And one sneaker hanging around on a lamp.

'Uh, hi there,' I said cautiously.

'Phloomph,' it said. It seemed to be eating something.

'How about a nice hot cup of instant?' I suggested.

With that, whoever-it-was sat up in a hurry, turned around, and stared at me with its mouth wide open. It had not swallowed what was in its mouth. A marshmallow. Since I have never in my entire life seen my mother eating a marshmallow, I begin to have a sneaking hunch that this was not my mother. It gulped and swallowed.

'A nice hot cup of *instant*?' it repeated. 'What are you? Crazy? You know I don't drink that stuff.'

It was Annabel all right. No doubt about it. Outside of the fact that Ma doesn't eat marshmallows and I do, there is the fact that if it was really Ma, she wouldn't ask me if I was crazy because she'd know I was Annabel thinking she was Ma. But if *she* was really Annabel too, no wonder she thought I was crazy. Any mother who asks her daughter if she wants a nice hot cup of instant has to be crazy.

'I was talking about a nice hot cup of instant oatmeal,' I said in my haughtiest voice, 'and I'll thank you not to eat marshmallows before breakfast. It spoils your appetite.'

'What appetite?' she said. 'I never have any appetite for all that vomitizing stuff you pile into me. Besides, I'm full up on marshmallows.' She patted her stomach.

I decided to give in because it was getting too late to argue.

'OK, Annabel, forget breakfast, just get yourself dressed.'

'But I can't get dressed,' she complained. 'I can't get dressed 'til I find my blue tights and I don't see where they are.' I didn't see where they were either but I found some red ones in between Book B and Book S of the Junior Britannica. (In my library, S comes after B and L follows that.)

'Why don't you wear red? Red would be nice,' I suggested in Ma's most reasonable voice. I should have known better.

'No,' she said, crossly, 'I want blue.' I looked around wildly, trying to remember where I'd put them last night. They were in the wastebasket.

'You are a living doll,' she said, blowing me several ballerina kisses. 'How can I possibly sank you for zis enormous favour you do for me?' She'd gone into her French routine. What a nut! At least she was in a good mood again. The thing about Annabel is that she usually changes her moods quickly and often. Today, I wasn't going to know what to expect, or when. What was going on in her head right now, I wondered. Maybe she was thinking about her homework and McGuirk the Jerk. If she wasn't, she should be!

'Annabel, what are you going to tell Miss McGuirk?' I asked.

'About what?' she said.

'About the English composition,' I said.

'You mean the English composition I was behind on?' she asked.

'Uh-huh,' I said.

'Oh, I handed that in early last week,' she said, looking me right in the eye. You want somebody to believe you, you always look 'em right in the eye. It's a slick trick of mine . . . works every time.

'Good girl,' I said, because that's what Ma would've said. And anyway, what did I care what went on in school? That was her problem, not mine.

Ape Face stood in the doorway, jacket on, earmuffs on, and a big, gooey smile all over his dumb face. Every day he's ready ahead of time, just to show me up, the fink!

'I'm all ready, Mommy, and I walked Max,' he said in his dumb voice. 'He did a big thing and two little things. Annabel better hurry or we're going to miss the bus.'

'If we do, it's because you're standing in my way,' she snarled. 'Get out of here, Ape Face, and don't talk to me.'

'I wasn't.'

'You are now! And don't!' she said, throwing on the rest of her clothes.

'I'm not!' he said.

'Ape Face, *shut* up!' she said. To tell the truth, both of them were getting on my nerves. I tried to remember what Ma did with us in the morning.

'All right, all right, all right, you two, that's enough of that,' I said, pushing them to the front door. So far, so good.

'And Annabel, I've told you a million times, don't call him Ape Face; his name is Ben.' Even better! I was beginning to sound more like Ma than Ma does.

'Bye-bye, darlings, have a nice day,' I said, holding the door open for them. But Ape Face just stood there. What was he waiting for, I wondered? Then a grotesque thought came to me. He was waiting to be kissed and I was going to have to do it. So I did – as quickly as possible. Actually, it wasn't too bad.

He smelled kind of nice. But I hoped he didn't expect it again at lunchtime. Annabel didn't expect it at all, she never does. Just as well. I would have felt funny kissing myself good-bye.

Four

Now that the kids were gone, the apartment was so quiet I could hear my own breathing. There were a few small noises: the sanitation truck grinding away down the street, Max lapping up water in the kitchen, Daddy clearing his throat and rustling the *Times* in the dining room; but they weren't noises I had to do anything about. It was what Ma calls a little peace and quiet to give her time to think. Ordinarily I hate peace and quiet; it's boring. But today . . .

Come to think of it, speaking of Ma, I'd been too busy to worry about it before (not that I was worried now, just curious) but if Annabel's mind was in Annabel's body, which it certainly seemed to be, and Annabel's mind was also in Ma's body, which it most definitely was (me is me, no matter what I look like), then where did Ma's mind get to? Somebody else's body, I suppose – but whose? If I were Ma, who would I be? Queen Elizabeth? Jackie Onassis? Gloria Steinem, Willa Cather? Or is Willa Cather dead? Yeah, I think she's dead.

Oh well, whoever she was, I hoped she was enjoying it and I hoped she wasn't going to be back too soon. At least until after English was over – I couldn't think of anything more hairy than turning back into myself in front of McGuirk. 'I hope she gives me a whole day,' I thought to myself. A day and a night, so I can stay up late.

I looked in Ma's datebook to see if she had anything nice planned. It was rather disappointing. Under Morning, it said buy more scotch; under Afternoon, it said '2.30' with a box around it – two-thirty where? Who with? She must keep all those things in her head, and now she's gone off with her head, the inside of it anyway, so whatever is happening at two-thirty, I'm just going to have to miss it, unfortunately.

Under Evening, it was blank. How about that! My first chance to have a good time and we're not going out to someone's house for dinner, or to a festive occasion. Phooey! And as for buying more scotch, how much was more? I looked in Ma's purse – it had seventeen dollars in it. Was that enough?

Daddy was still reading the paper in the dining room. I'd have to ask him.

'Hi, darling,' he said. 'Kids get off all right?'

'Oh sure,' I said. 'Listen, I was just wondering . . .'

'Hmmnn?' he said, still reading the paper.

'We seem to be out of scotch so I thought I'd get some more.'

'Good idea,' he said. 'While you're at it, pick up a bourbon and two gin – we're always out of gin.'

'Maybe I don't have enough money for all that,' I said, doubtfully. Daddy put down the paper and looked at me for a minute. Then he sighed. Not a long, teed-off sigh, more of a short, soft grunt.

'Ellen,' he said, 'I gave you fifty dollars yesterday. Where did it all go?'

I was beginning to not like this conversation. How did I know what she spent her money on yesterday!

'I'm not sure,' I said, 'but I only have seventeen dollars left.'

'Just think about it for a minute,' he said, in the same voice he uses on me-Annabel when I can't do a maths problem – patient/impatient.

'The butter and egg man? He gets paid on Thursday,' I said hopefully.

'OK, that's about seven dollars. What else?'

'Five dollars for more vacuum cleaner bags?'

27

'All righty, seven for eggs and five for what's got to be a three-year supply of vacuum cleaner bags, and you have seventeen left, so what happened to the other twenty-one?'

How does he *do* that so fast in his head?

'I'm not too good at this,' I mumbled.

'After fifteen years of marriage, that's hardly news to me,' he said. It may not have been news to him but it was certainly news to *me*. No wonder I'm so lousy at maths. Like mother like daughter.

He went on, 'Now think, Ellen. What happened to the other twenty-one? You didn't spend it on yourself; you never do. Did you buy something for the children?'

That reminded me. 'I bought a new raincoat and boots for Annabel.'

'What was the matter with the old raincoat and the old boots?'

'Nothing was the matter with them. She just lost them, that's all.'

Very slowly and very quietly, Daddy said, 'She just lost them, did she?' and then he got mad at both of us. He said Annabel was careless and sloppy and I was too easy on her. He said this was the second raincoat and boots Annabel had lost this year (Actually, it was the third.) and that I couldn't go on spending money on her like there was no tomorrow and didn't I know money was scarce all over.

Well, maybe Ma knew all that, but I didn't. How could I? They never talked about those things in front of me.

For a minute nobody said anything, which was nice. Maybe now was the time for me to leave the room. I stood up.

'And while we're at it, Ellen, there's one more thing.' I sat down again. 'Annabel's camp is going to cost nine hundred dollars. Not counting equipment. Why does Annabel have to go to camp?'

'She doesn't have to, but she's dying to,' I said. I really was dying to. My three best friends were going. Was Daddy going to say I couldn't go? They promised! They absolutely had to let me, I'd die! — Cool it Annabel, cool it, you catch more bees with honey or whatever that saying is.

'Bill, camp means a great deal to Annabel. She's been counting on it. And we gave our promise.'

'That's only half accurate, my love. You apparently gave her *your* promise while I wasn't around.'

'But for three weeks, she kept begging and pleading and carrying on, and then one day when I was busy on the phone, she said, "Ma, just say yes," so I said yes. She tricked me into it.'

Daddy looked at me for a second and then he did

something he often does with me but I've never seen him do it with Ma. He put his hand out, palm up, on the dining-room table, and waited for me to put my hand in his. So I did.

Then he said, 'Ellen, old girl, you've been had. We've both been had.'

'How do you mean?' I asked.

'Look,' he said, 'I know you love Annabel and you want her to be happy. And you know I love Annabel and I want her to be happy, too, but what about us being happy together?'

What on earth did he mean by that?

'But we *are* happy, aren't we? *Aren't we?*' I asked again. Maybe they weren't, which would be awful, but I didn't see what it had to do with me-Annabel going to camp.

'I'm talking about together as a family. What happened to our nice little plan to rent a house in the country for July so all four of us could get away?'

'You mean if Annabel goes to camp, we can't do that? Is that what you mean?'

He nodded his head, tapped his forehead with one finger, and smiled a smirky smile at me.

'Gee,' I said.

'Mmn,' he said.

'Gee, I'm awfully sorry,' I said.

'Me too,' he said. This wasn't getting us anywhere. I'd have to think of something better.

'I guess I blew it,' I said. He sighed again, this time a big, long sigh, and I knew the worst was over. A good thing, too. I was getting twitchy. We both stood up.

'Just do me one favour, huh, Ellen?'

'Sure, anything, what?' I said.

'Don't make any more promises to Annabel without checking with me.'

'It's a deal,' I said, sticking out my hand. He didn't seem to know what to do with it so I pretended I was picking a fluff off his collar.

'Can I ask a favour of you?' I said.

'Sure thing,' he said.

'Well, we have nothing on for tonight. Could we go out to dinner and go to a movie?' If he didn't say yes I was in a lot of trouble because I could fake my way through breakfast but dinner was something else again. Besides, I love movies.

'Super idea,' he said. 'What's playing at the local?'

' "Brucey and Betsy". I hear it's terrific.'

'I also hear it's a pretty dirty flick,' he said.

'That's what I meant,' said I, cool as a cucumber.

'It's OK by me,' he said, looking at his watch. 'Listen, I've got to go or I'm going to be late. Get the sitter, figure out the movie schedule and where you want to go for dinner, and I'll call you later. Also, here's another twenty — two scotch, two gin, one bourbon, and is Mrs Schmauss coming today!'

'Let's see. Today's Friday? Yes, why?'

'Don't let her touch my shirts. She may be a good cleaner but she's a crummy laundress. Be a good girl and you do them, though, because I'm almost out. Good-bye, I'm late, I love you,' and out he went, slamming the front door behind him.

What a cute man!

Five

IMAGINE letting that poor cute man run almost out of shirts! I decided the first thing to do, before I even turned on the boob tube or picked out my dress for tonight, was those shirts. I found them in our (their?) bathroom hamper along with some other stuff (you know, the usual – socks, a couple of sweaters, a bra, some panty hose, pyjamas, a terry-cloth wrapper). When I carried it all into the kitchen, it seemed like a full load, but we have a great big machine. There was still room for more. Not wanting to waste electricity (*Our* generation *cares* about the environment.), I threw in a few other grimy goodies: P.F. Fliers belonging to Ape Face, my shirt from the Army & Navy Store, shaggy rug belonging to Max. A cup and a half of New Improved Fosphree, three quarters of a cup of Clorex, punch up the hot water dial, and away we go. Nothing to it.

I found a bowl of leftover macaroni in the fridge and I was just about to sit down and watch 'The Little Rascals' when the doorbell rang. Not expecting anybody and not wishing to be robbed on this, the most splendid day of my life, I peeked through the burglar hole . . . and almost fainted dead away. On the other side of the door stood Boris Harris!

Boris Harris is fourteen, he has chestnut hair and hazel eyes. I don't know how tall he is but it's a good three inches more than I am, and whatever he weighs is just perfect. He lives in our building, he is beautiful, and I love him.

'And he is standing outside our door right this minute holding a spaghetti sieve, and how am I going to handle the situation?' I asked myself. 'With charm and sophistication,' I answered myself, and with that I hid the bowl of macaroni in a wastebasket, and flung open the door.

'Why, good morning, *Boris*!' I said. 'What a lovely surp*rise*!'

'I cabe to returd your collader,' said Boris.

'That's very sweet of you,' I said.

'It was by buther's idea because it was by buther who borrowed it,' said Boris.

'Ah well, yes, I see what you mean,' I said, 'but in any case, why don't you come in for a minute. The

34

hall is no place to be standing in a negligee, don't you agree?'

'Doh, I guess dot,' said Boris, stepping over the threshold (What *took* him so long?), 'but I cad ohdly stay a biddit – by buther is expectig be hobe.'

'Poor Boris, that's a perfectly dreadful cold you've got there. Do you ever take Vitamin C? Let me get you some Vitamin C.'

'Please dohd bother, Brs Andrews, I dohd . . .'

'It's no bother at all,' I shouted over my shoulder as I galloped to the kitchen. 'Why don't you sit down in the living room and make yourself comfortable? I'm coming right back.'

I did come right back, but it took me a minute to find him because, dear God, do you know where he was? Standing in the doorway of my-Annabel's room, wide-eyed and slack-jawed. Slack-jawed could be due to the cold, but wide-eyed, I'm afraid, was due to something else.

'Who lives *there*?' he said, wrinkling his adorable red nose.

'My son, Ben,' I said, closing the door firmly.

'With a cadopy bed ad a *doll* house?'

'Yes, with a canopy bed and a dollhouse,' I said. 'My son is a very peculiar little boy.'

'I'll say,' agreed Boris. 'He is also a slob.'

'Right on!' I said with enthusiasm. 'Here, take your Vitamin C and then we can play a game or something. You want to?'

'Sure,' said Boris, and we played Nok Hockey for twenty minutes on the floor of the living room. He won, which was fine with me.

'You did very well for a lady, though. Whed was the last tibe you played?'

'Yesterday. As a matter of fact, I play every day with Annabel. If you think I'm good, you should see her. She's great. Not as good as you, of course, but she'd give you a run for your money. You ought to come down and play with Annabel sometime.'

'I'd rather play with you,' said Boris.

'She also plays gin rummy, Monopoly, Dirty Water – that's a pollution game; she's very into the environment thing, you know – and chess.

'*Plus*, it's all I can do to stop her from reading – everything from Willa Cather to Salinger to Ian Fleming – *plus* a super collection of records – everything from country and western . . .'

'I hate coudtry ad westerd,' said Boris.

'– to mostly classical and one or two show albums. Actually, she only has one country and western. Some boy gave it to her.

'You know, Boris,' I continued, 'lately, Annabel has completely changed. She is no longer the same person who cut your scalp open with a tin shovel in the playground five years ago.'

'Four,' said Boris.

'OK, four,' I conceded. 'Anyway, if you saw her now, you wouldn't even recognize her.'

'Does she still have braces?' he asked.

'Well –' I began.

'Because if she still has braces, I'd recognize her.'

'However, she's much nicer now than she used to be,' I said.

'I'm sure she is,' said Boris amiably. 'But Mrs Andrews, to be perfectly frank, that's not saying much.'

Thud. Long silence.

'Mrs Andrews,' said Boris, 'it's not your fault that Annabel is the way she is. She's probably what they call a bad seed.'

I stared at him. Then he got to his feet. I got to my feet.

'I think I'd better be going now,' he said, 'but I want to thank you for a wonderful time.'

'That's OK, Boris, you come on down and visit whenever you want. You don't even have to call. Just come. Maybe we'll play some Dirty Water.'

'I'd like that,' said Boris. 'Most grown-ups don't want to play games. They're too busy or something. But then, you're not the same as most grown-ups.

You're . . .' he looked at me carefully for a moment and then shrugged his shoulders and grinned.

'Anyway,' he said, 'thanks, and thanks for the Vitamin C. That must be very zappy stuff. Did you notice my cold is completely gone?' And with that, he opened the front door and left before I even had a chance to say I hadn't noticed. Which I hadn't. Oh, the pain of it all, the naked aching pain!

I fished the bowl of macaroni out of the waste-basket, and turned on the living-room television set. I was hoping to find a good cartoon, but it was after ten and I couldn't even find a bad cartoon. I suppose they figure all the kids are in school and grown-ups like to watch other kinds of shows. Not very thought-ful of them. What about a poor little sick kid who has to stay home, or a poor little kid who's changed into her mother for the day. Not even one 'Road Runner'? No sir. One ladies' panel show, one sewing show, 'Romper Room', one show that looked good but it was all in Spanish, and a show called 'Swing and Sway with Jean Dupray, Physical Fitness the Real Fun Way'. That seemed like the best of the bunch, but just as I was beginning to get the hang of the swinging and swaying (which was easier for old Jean than for me because she was wearing a tank suit over tights and I was wearing Ma's long silk thing), there was the most staggeringly horrible noise in the kitchen. Right away, I knew it had to be the washing machine, and it took all the guts I had to go in there and look. Not that there was much to see – just bubbles – but the clatter and bang was enough to make you deaf for life. I was just about to turn it off before it went into the spin cycle – because it was mad as a hornet now, but when it started spinning it would probably break loose and chase me around the room – when the phone rang.

'Hell,' I said. Too late. The spin cycle had begun. Last year, our class took a trip to an old car grave-yard – a big crane throws dead cars into a pile and then a compressor thing mashes them all together into one large, tutti-frutti mess. All I can tell you is that compared to the racket in the kitchen, a trip to an old car graveyard is like a trip to Grant's Tomb (where we also went last year).

'Hello, hello, hello,' I shouted. Couldn't hear a word. I put the phone down in the kitchen and picked it up in the hall. Couldn't hear a word there either because all the noise in the kitchen was coming through from one phone to the other. Stupid of me, wasn't it?

'Hello? Wait a minute, hang on, I gotta hang up in the kitchen,' I said and ran back again, but now there were suds all over the floor; it was like Christmas in Vermont. And the machine was dead as a doornail.

'Couldn't you pick some other day to have a breakdown?' I said, giving it a kick.

'I mean what was the matter with yesterday, when my mother was around? If you were going to shake yourself to death, why didn't you do it then? You had to do it on her day off? Come on, now, shape up!' I said, giving it another kick and a hit. Sometimes if you hit a machine a couple of times you can get it going again, at least that's what I do with my record player. But this thing was a goner. I could tell.

'Thanks for nothing,' I said. 'And as for you,' I said to Max, who was sampling the suds, 'you lap up any more of that stuff and you're going to be good and sick.'

I looked up the washing-machine-repair number and picked up the phone to call the place, and would you *believe* it? there was no dialling tone! I hung up and picked it up again. Still no dialling tone. On the third try, I picked it up in the middle of somebody saying hello. Crossed wires again. It happens all the time. I took a deep breath and then very slowly and distinctly, I said, 'Madame, I think we have crossed wires. You are in on my line. If you will simply hang up and I will simply hang up you will be able to reach your party and I will be able to reach my party.'

The other end cleared its throat, and then very slowly and distinctly said, 'Five minutes ago you asked me to hang on. Now you want me to hang up. Have you gone absolutely out of your mind?'

'Oh, my goodness!' I said, 'Are you the person I was talking to before? Yes of course you are, I never hung up out there, did I? How idiotic of me. I'm *terribly* sorry! Listen, lemme just hang up in the hall and I'll be right . . .'

'Oh, no you don't!' screamed the voice. 'That's what you said the last time. I'm not waiting one more minute. I have cream on my face and I've been waiting to get into the bath for over an hour!'

'Well, what's that got to do with me?' I said. 'Who is this anyway?'

'Ellen Jean, this is your mother. Who in blue blazes did you think it was?'

Now that's what I call a lulu of a boo-boo, not to recognize your own grandmother (or mother, as the case may be).

'Oh, Mother,' I said, 'I do apologize, but it was so noisy in here on account of the machine. Anyway, how are you?'

'Oh, I'm all right, I suppose, but as you know, dear, I don't take my bath until after your call because it's so inconvenient to have to get *out* of the bath and chilly. So I do wish you'd remember to call me exactly at nine. Could you remember to do that, dear?'

'Sure, Mother, sure,' I said.

'Thank you, dear,' she said, 'Oh, and Ellen Jean, do you and Bill have any plans for the Fourth of July weekend?'

'You want to know now, in February, what we're doing on the Fourth of July?' She's too much!

She said the reason she wanted to know *now* was that if we weren't coming (the house in Larchmont) she wanted to line up some other people because I knew how lonely it had been since Dad took sick and passed on. (If there's anything I can't stand, it's 'took sick' and 'passed on' or 'passed away'. What's the matter with just plain 'died'?)

So I looked in Ma's date book which didn't have anything down for the Fourth of July, and then I got a brainstorm.

'Mother,' I said, 'Not only are we free for the weekend of the Fourth, but how would you like to have us for the whole month? That way, you wouldn't be lonely, and Bill and I could get out of the hot city . . .'

'I think that would be just wonderful,' she said, 'but what about the children? There are only two guest bedrooms, and surely Ben and Annabel are getting too old to share a room.'

'Didn't I tell you?' I said gaily. 'Annabel's going to camp this summer. There's plenty of room in your house and Bill will be thrilled.'

'What accounts for his change of heart, I wonder? Ah well, ours not to question why, is it now?' I didn't have the faintest idea of what she was talking about but thought it best to agree with her anyway. Then I explained I had to get off the phone to call about the washing machine, and we both made kiss-kiss noises at each other and said good-bye.

Annabel Andrews, when you put your mind to it, you have a mind like a steel trap! Camp was saved; Daddy's July was saved; now if I could just figure out how to save the machine and the shirts, I'd be ahead of the game.

Six

WOULD you be interested in knowing how long it took me to get the washing-machine-repair number to answer? Fifteen minutes. Might you also be interested in knowing how far I got with the man I finally talked to, after he kept me on hold for another five minutes?

I won't bore you with the whole conversation, just one or two highlights. First I gave him my name and address, and then I said, 'My washing machine broke down this morning. I have six children, two in nappies, and I'm desperate. Please, could you come over and fix it – now?'

He said, 'First I gotta get the particulars. What make machine?'

'It's a Miracle Maid.'

'Miracle Maid. OK. Which type?'

'Top sider.'

'Lady, you want a sneaker repaired, go to a shoe
tore. I'm a very busy man – no time for jokes. You
don't mean top sider, you mean top loader. So *say*
top loader.'

'Top loader.'

'Now we're getting somewhere. So how long you
had this top loader?'

'Wait a minute, you're getting me all mixed up. I
only said top loader because you said, "Say top
loader." I don't have a top loader, I have a side
loader. I mean front loader. A broken front loader
which I desperately need you to come and fix, *today*.'

You know what he said? He said, 'I'll have a man
up there a week from Wednesday, lady,' and hung
up. Zilch is how far I got.

I chewed off a couple of fingernails and then wan-
dered into Ma's closet to try on a few things. I was
just admiring myself in a black velvet pants suit
(which looked very nice, I thought) when the doorbell rang. Could it possibly be beautiful Boris Harris
coming back for another round of Nok Hockey? I
peeked through the burglar peephole. No, it could
not. It was Rose Schmauss, the cleaning lady. A
dismal comedown.

Mrs Schmauss I don't know very well. She usually
arrives after I've gone to school and she's gone before
I get home. Once in a while she baby-sits – I'd have to

ask her about tonight. As far as looks go, let me put it to you this way: she's the next closest thing to a rhinoceros, with a voice that could shatter glass, and she smells funny.

'How *are* you, Mrs Andrews? What a precious outfit. Going out to lunch, I imagine.' Was she asking me or telling me? Maybe she knew something I didn't know. Maybe that's what two-thirty with a box around it meant. A late lunch date with somebody. But who?

'What's *your* guess Mrs Schmauss?' I asked coyly.

'I'd guess you have a rawndyvoo with a secret lover, right?' she said, poking me in the ribs with her fat finger. The dirty bird!

'Wrong,' said I, promptly. 'I'm on my way to the liquor store.'

'In *that* you're going to the liquor store? A ladies' luncheon maybe, but to go around the corner in?'

It's none of her business what I go around the corner in. I know just as well as she does people don't wear velvet with rhinestone buttons in the morning, but they do wear them in the evening and that's what I was dressed for. I don't see why grown-ups keep changing their clothes all day long. An old rag to do the breakfast dishes in (heck, I forgot to do the breakfast dishes; oh well, Mrs Schmauss could) a skirt to go to the store in, a dress to go to lunch in, pants to go to the park in, and velvet and rhinestones to go to dinner in. If you count in and out of your nightgown twice, that makes six changes. What a bore! I like to get into one thing and stay in it.

'I'm quite comfortable the way I am,' I said icily.

'Honey!' she said, pinching my cheek, 'No offence intended. If it makes you happy, it makes me happy.'

'I'm happy,' I said.

'Good, great! That's what I like to hear,' she boomed. 'Now where do you want me to start today? In the kitchen, I'll bet.'

'You bet absolutely right,' I said happily, following her down the hall. 'I have had a simply hideous morning. I haven't even got to the breakfast dishes.'

'Oh?' she said, glaring at me over her fat shoulder. 'How come?'

'Because the washing machine broke and there are suds all over the floor.'

'That so,' she said. By now we were in the kitchen.

'I don't see no suds,' she said. I didn't see no suds either, just a little water on the floor. They must have melted.

'How do you know this machine is broke? It don't look broke to me.' She leaned down and squinted into it.

'Because it made this awful noise, and then it stopped altogether. And there *were* a lot of suds.'

'It stopped because it was through,' she said, pointing to the dial. 'See? It says off. Off means through.'

'No kidding,' I said.

'Hon*ey*!' she said again, 'No offence, I'm sure. Just trying to be helpful. Now let's take a look what's going on inside.'

She opened the machine door and began unloading all the stuff into the laundry sink.

'Well, no *wonder*!' she said. 'You're gonna cram your shirts *and* your rugs *and* your hose *and* your *sneakers*, and some little tin things – what are these little tin things? oh, they're jacks – *and* your jacks all in together, not to mention you used too much soap, and *that*,' she said triumphantly, '*that* explains your noise and your suds.'

'Yeah, I guess it might,' I said. 'That's what comes of letting Annabel help with the laundry. Those must be her jacks. Sweet thing was only trying to be helpful.'

'A genuine first!' said Mrs Schmauss, snorting through her sinuses. 'Since when did she decide to be helpful? Or is today your birthday?' I decided to let that one pass.

'All right, Mrs Schmauss,' I said, 'if you want to start finishing up the laundry now, please, but never mind doing the shirts today.'

'Today? Whaddya mean *today*? I never did the

48

shirts before, I should sunly stop doing them *now?*

'Lissen, honey,' she said, waving her fat finger under my nose, 'when I come to work for you what was it, two, three months ago? – we agreed on a couple things I don't do. Number one is *I don't do no men's shirts.*'

'And number two is?' I could hardly wait to hear.

'Mrs Andrews, we have to go into that again?'

'If it's not asking too much, Mrs Schmauss, I demand to know – number two is *what?*'

'Don't holler on me, Missy, I'm not one of your coloured!'

I blinked at her. 'That is a disgusting thing to say,' I shouted. 'Hollering has nothing to do with colouring. And we don't call them coloured, we call them . . .'

'Yah, yah, yah. All you liberals make me sick. I know what you call 'em; you call 'em black, right? Well *I* call 'em no-goodniks.'

'And what do you call *you?*' I whispered. 'You won't do this and you won't do that and you won't even tell me what you won't do. TELL ME WHAT IS THAT NUMBER TWO THING YOU WON'T DO!'

But Mrs Schmauss was already halfway down the hall to the bedrooms.

'Come back here, where are you going?' I said.

'I don't have to tell you, I'll *show* you,' said Mrs Schmauss, turning the doorknob of Annabel's door and kicking the door with her foot.

'Holy Mother Of God, it's worse than usual!' she muttered.

'Number two is I do not pick up pigpens. That honour is reserved for the mother of the pig.

'Oh, beg pardon,' she went on in this smarmy tone, 'we don't call her a pig, do we? We call her "a little thoughtless", or "a little forgetful". Well I call her a little pig!

'Howdya like this?' she said, pointing to the red tights between Book B and Book S. 'And this?' – she pointed to a marshmallow impaled on a magenta Mongol. 'I suppose you can't call this a coloured pencil, can you? And you can't call it a black pencil, so whaddya gonna call it? A Negro pencil? Ha!

'And how dya love this melted candle wax on your best bone china, and the apple core under the bed, and the underpanties under the bed . . .'

'They're perfectly clean underpants!' I said indignantly.

'But under the bed. Is that where they belong? Under the bed?

'Lemme tell you something, Mrs Andrews. That kid's got no discipline, and a kid that's got no discipline is the fault of the mother and the father.'

'Not necessarily,' said I.

'Oh yes, oh *yes*. I've seen it time and again. You liberal folks are the ones turn out the troublemakers in this country. She'll be on drugs before you know it.'

Rose Schmauss, you are one demented lady, I thought to myself. The whole conversation was so wild, I wasn't even mad anymore.

'Oh?' I said. 'What makes you think so?'

'Well,' she said, 'remember Wednesday you asked me if I'd seen the half bottle of gin that was on the bar on Monday? That was probably your way of accusing me of drinking your liquor.'

'It probably was,' I said. No wonder she smells funny. People who don't smoke have a better sense of smell than people who smoke. Ma smokes like a chimney, but by Wednesday, even she must have wised up.

'That's what I thought,' said Mrs Schmauss smugly, 'but now I'm going to tell you something.' She leaned toward me.

'I'm not saying I wouldn't take an occasional nip or two, but only my own hooch. I wouldn't touch nobody else's. She's never gonna admit it, but you know who's been drinking your gin?'

'Annabel,' I said. My Lord. The woman was crazed!

'You said it; I didn't,' said Mrs Schmauss.

So then I did something that gave me such pleasure, I can't begin to tell you. In a grave and thoughtful voice, I said, 'Mrs Schmauss, honey, you're fired.'

Seven

WHAT happened before I finally got her out of the apartment isn't worth describing in detail. Briefly, though, she asked me why I was firing her. I told her she was a liar and a drunk and prejudiced, which were not qualities I admired. She told me I was prejudiced — against Germans. I said I thought she was American. She said her grandfather was born in Germany. I said I had nothing against her grandfather. I didn't even know him. She said how could I know him, he was dead? I said I was sorry to hear it, was she very fond of him? She said she never knew him either, he died before she was born. In that case, I said, would she please give me the key to the apartment — which didn't have anything to do with anything but she was too far gone to notice. She gave me the key. I thanked her. She left.

The minute the twelve o'clock whistle blew, Max

ran to the front door, ready to go out. Pavlov would have been delighted with him. Even I was kind of pleased; it gave me an excuse to get out of the apartment, and besides, I could buy the liquor at the same time.

For February, it was quite a nice day, and I took my time going to the corner. Had a friendly chat with the liquor store man, in which I warned him not to expect us to buy as much gin in the future, and told him about Mrs Schmauss. He tsk-tsked a lot, gave me my change, and asked if I didn't want the bottles delivered – the boy could bring them right over. I said no thank you, I would just as soon carry them. If I'd had any idea what was going to happen next, I would have just as soon *not* carried them. I would, in fact, have been better off dead.

Up the block, across the street from our building, a crowd had collected. Also a police car. Now, she never lets me stop at accidents. I've told her a million times I only throw up at the sight of my *own* blood, but she hurries me along, saying, 'Don't look, don't look!' This was my big chance.

Whoever said 'curiosity killed the cat' must have had me in mind, because when I finally pushed my way to the centre of the circle, me and the dog and the five bottles of liquor, what'd I see but the blue-eyed ape himself, screaming and crying at the top of his lungs for 'Mommy'. 'I want my Mommy!' Ai-yi, I forgot to meet the bus!

You don't know how close I came to slipping quietly away again. After all, I wasn't his real mother anyway. Why not let the fuzz take him to the station house and feed him ice cream cones, and when she was ready to claim her own bod again (and give me back mine), she could go pick him up. Why not? I'll tell you why not. Because the little brat spotted me, that's why not.

'Oh Mommy, Mommy!' he sobbed, throwing his arms around my stomach, at the same time clobbering me in the small of the back with I don't know what – I couldn't see it.

'All right, I'm here, aren't I? Pipe down, cool it, that's en*ough*!' I snarled; but public opinion was running against me. People were saying things like, 'Aw, the poor little fellow!' and 'Vot kinda Mama is dot, I esk you?' and 'That unfeeling woman should be reported to the ASPCA.'

'C,' I said over my shoulder.

'Oh, a spic,' said another voice. 'She said *si*.'

'We don't call them spics, we call them Puerto Ricans or Spanish-speaking Americans, and I said ASPCC.'

'OK, Officer, report her to them,' said the author of the unfeeling-woman line.

'Ladies, ladies, would you let me handle this, please?' said the cop. He unwrapped Ape Face's arms from around my middle (which, thank heavens, gave me a chance to set the five bottles down on the sidewalk – my arms were killing me), and then he kneeled down, saying, 'Now, sonny, tell Officer Plonchik; is this your mother?'

'Of course I'm his mother. You heard him call me Mommy. Who else would I be?' Who else indeed? His sister, for one.

'Ma'am, please let him speak for himself. We have to have a positive identification. Once again, sonny, is this your mother?'

'Yes,' said Ape Face.

The cop straightened up. 'Well, Ma'am, it's a wise son that knows his own mother, as you might say.'

'*You* might say it, I wouldn't,' I said. 'Can we go now?'

'In a minute. I'd like to ask you a few questions, if you don't mind. Have you ever abandoned this child before?'

'I didn't abandon him. I simply went to the liquor store and was late meeting the bus.'

'Liquor is more important than your son, is that it?'

'Officer, I've never been late before. Ask him. Ask him if I've ever been late before.' I poked the Ape.

'No,' said Ape Face.

'Well, all right, then, but you're a very fortunate woman. He might have been killed crossing the street, or been abducted.' (No such luck, I thought sourly.)

'So *ciao*, Officer, see you around,' I said.

'Thank you for taking care of me, sir,' said Mealy-mouth.

'You're old enough to take care of yourself,' I said, as soon as we were out of earshot. 'When you didn't see me there, why didn't you come on home alone?'

'And cross the street?' he squeaked. 'You always told me if you didn't come, just to wait at the corner for you and *never* to cross the street.'

'It's time you learned. Right now. Quick, tell me, what colour does the light say now?' I wanted to make sure he wasn't colour-blind.

'Green.'

'Good. Now scram.'

'Hold my helicopter, I don't want to cross with my hands full,' he said and handed me his ... helicopter? This is a helicopter? This is two hunks of nailed-together wood with three twisted pipe cleaners on top. This is also what clobbered me in the small of my back.

'Hey, Mom, I did it! I did it!' he shouted, jumping

up and down on the other side of the street. 'Did you see me?'

'Yes,' I lied, and against the light, I raced across the street, with the dog and the five bottles of liquor and the helicopter.

'You shouldn't do that. It's dangerous,' he said.

'Grown-ups get to do it if they want to,' I said. 'And anyway, mind your own business.'

He flashed me a quick look. 'I'm sorry. Here, I can carry my own helicopter.' He took it from me and didn't say another word until we were upstairs in the apartment.

I went right to the kitchen to start washing the soap out of Daddy's shirts and the rest of the stuff. It was ghastly work. Ape Face sat on a stool and watched me.

Finally, after about ten minutes, he said, 'Aren't I going to get some lunch?'

'When I'm good and ready,' I snapped. 'I'm busy doing something. Can't you see?' From the look on his face, I think I had him pretty scared, but he squeezed his hands into fists, took a big, brave breath, and in a very little voice asked me where Mrs Schmauss was.

'I fired her,' I said, rinsing out a P.F. Flier.

'You mean she's not coming any more? Not ever?' he whispered. Oh boy, if he starts crying again, I'll kill him! I thought to myself. I rinsed out the other sneaker.

'No,' I said, calmly and firmly, 'not ever.' There was a second of silence, and then behind my back there was such an explosion of screaming and shouting and pounding on the counter, and the dog started barking, and when I turned around, that lunatic was tearing out the kitchen door, followed by the dog. Twice around the apartment they went, barking and shouting – for *joy*, mind you, for joy! – until they were both out of breath, and then the Ape sat right back down on the same kitchen stool and just grinned at me.

'I take it you didn't like her either,' I said.

'Like her! Oh Ma, I hate her. She talks cross all the time and she smells bad, and mostly I hate her because she says Annabel is a spoiled brat and a pig . . .'

'I heard that once already, today. I don't have to hear it again.' Mealymouthed hypocrite, I bet he loves repeating all those things about Annabel.

'Well, anyway,' he went on, 'that's the mostly reason why I hate Mrs Schmauss.'

'Oooh, I'll just bet,' I said, planting my hands on my hips and glaring at him with my eyebrows raised.

'I'll just bet!' I said again, and turned back to the sink to pick rug fuzz out of the drain.

'But it is,' he insisted. 'It honestly is.' I heaved the

gob of rug fuzz at the garbage (missed), dried my hands on the – whoops – on the velvet pants suit, and sat down opposite the Ape at the counter.

'Listen,' I said, 'lemme get something straight. The main reason you hate Mrs Schmauss is because Mrs Schmauss hates Annabel, is that right?'

'Yes,' he said. From the tone of his voice, you'd think I'd asked him if he was sure one and one made two.

'Look, stupid-o,' I said. 'You're not making any sense. You hate Mrs Schmauss because Mrs Schmauss hates Annabel; but Annabel hates *you*, so what do you care if Mrs Schmauss hates her?'

'I just do,' he said, twiddling the top of his hair with one finger – he does that when he gets embarrassed. When he was littler, he used to do it in his sleep and once he got his finger so snarled up in the hair, Ma had to cut the hair off to get the finger out. Stupid jerk!

'But it doesn't make any sense to hate somebody who hates somebody who hates you. I mean, if you want to hate Mrs Schmauss for other reasons, OK, but the person you should really hate is Annabel.'

'I know it,' he said, twiddling away. 'I try. But I just can't.'

'Why not?' I asked.

'Dunno. Just can't,' he said. Twiddle, twiddle, twiddle.

'Cut that out or you'll get your finger stuck again. Come on, now, tell me why not. If she's that great, what's so great about her? Tell me one thing. Just one.'

'OK. Let's see. One thing. Uh ... OK, yeah, I got one thing. Do you remember that time a long, long time ago when you and Daddy came home and said, "What's all that white stuff out on the street? It looks like it's been hailing." '

'You mean when you and Annabel threw the gobs of Kleenex and she said it was all your fault because it was your idea and besides you threw most of them, so you got punished and she didn't?'

'Yeah, that's the time,' he said happily. 'That was really great.'

'You are a complete loon,' I said. 'It was Annabel's idea and Annabel threw most of them – you only threw two – so it was Annabel's fault and you got punished. What's so great about that, and what's so great about a person who pulls that kind of finky trick? That's not what I call great.'

'Aw, Ma, you don't understand. I don't mind getting punished. It doesn't happen very often anyway' (that's for sure) 'but we had such a good time doing it and I wouldn't of been able to reach where you keep the Kleenex by myself. I wouldn't of even thought of doing it by myself.

'See, Annabel gets these great ideas of things to do and I never get *any*. She is the smartest person I know.' I wondered if he really meant it about the ideas or if he was just looking for a polite way to rat on me.

'What are some of her other ideas that you think are so terrific? What other bad things does she do?'

'Aren't I going to get some lunch soon?' he said, sliding off the stool and jiggling up and down. 'I'm awful hungry because the graham crackers didn't go around twice. Also, I have to go to the bathroom.' He ran out of the kitchen before I had a chance to ask him anything else, so I decided he might be a lot of other rotten things but he wasn't a rotten rat.

As I think I said before, I'm not much of a cook, so for the Ape's lunch, I took a bunch of stuff out of the fridge and put it on the counter for him to choose from. Plus the bowl of cold macaroni. When he came back from the bathroom, he looked at the macaroni and last night's damp salad and a couple of cold meatballs and half a thing of yogurt.

'Cleaning out the fridge?' he asked.

'This is a pick-up lunch. Pick up anything you want and throw the rest out,' I said.

'No lamb chop or baked potato or string beans?' he asked.

'Not unless you want to cook it yourself.'

'Nah, I hate hot lunches,' he said. 'They make me sick.'

'Me, too,' I said, and for a while nobody said anything. We ate the macaroni with our fingers out of the bowl. Then Ape Face asked if it was all right to put some grape jelly on the meat balls, they would taste nice that way, and I let him.

Then he said, 'Another good thing about Annabel is she's very popular.'

'Who with?' I asked.

'With everybody in my class,' he said.

'Big deal,' I said scornfully. 'A whole mob of six year olds. Wowee!'

'She's also very popular with *her* class,' he said.

'With the boys?' Maybe he knew something I didn't know.

'Oh, not the *boys* ... just the girls,' he said.

'Well, what's the matter with her? Why don't the boys like her? She's not bad looking.' I leaned over and peered into his face. 'Do you think she's bad looking?'

'I think she's beautiful,' he said, 'but I guess it's

her braces. Not everybody likes braces. I don't know why. I love braces. When I get that old I hope I have them.'

'With your luck, you won't need them,' I said.

'That's what I'm afraid of,' he said, 'because then she's gonna hate me even more than she does now.

'Ma, why does she hate me so much?'

'Because you're a good little boy who never gets into any trouble, that's why. There is nothing more annoying in the whole entire world than a little blue-eyed saint with perfect teeth who is always on time and who never has a messy room!'

'Do you hate me, too?' asked Ape Face nervously.

'Oh, don't be a jackass! I'm just trying to explain why Annabel hates you. I mean I couldn't swear to it or anything, but if I was Annabel I wouldn't like having a brother who was cute-looking *and* neat.'

'But I can't help those things! I can't help what I look like, I don't even care what I look like – and about being neat. I can't help that either.

'Listen!' he shouted. 'Do you know something? If I thought she'd like me any better, I'd be messy. I've even tried being messy. Once I took all my piled-up blocks and the books in the shelves and the big bag of marbles and the Legos and flinged them all in the middle of the room so Annabel wouldn't be the only one getting in trouble, and you know what happened? That stinky Mrs Schmauss said I was too young to know any better and picked everything up! So no matter what I do, Annabel keeps on hating me.' His voice went into a wail and he hit the counter so hard the macaroni bowl jumped and his face was red and sweaty from yelling.

'Hey, hey, hey! Cool it. Calm down. Maybe you're exaggerating a little.'

He calmed down all right, but he also started to cry.

'No,' he said, in between sobs, 'she really hates me.'

Oh ook, oh cripes, oh crum, what to do now? I'd better make a joke. 'Well then, why don't you just hate her right back?'

'I told you before,' he said, 'I try. But you can't hate someone and love them at the same time. Whoever heard of that?'

'Have a Kleenex,' I said. 'Your tears are getting in your mouth. Must taste lousy after grape jelly.'

'Can you, Ma? Can you hate someone and love them at the same time?'

'I didn't used to think so, Ape Face, but I guess maybe you can.' Maybe you can.

It's funny how little kids don't blow their noses very well. I helped him, and asked him if he was feeling better now. He said yes, thank you, he was.

And then he said, 'That's the first time you ever called me Ape Face.' Another lulu of a boo-boo. I told him I was terribly sorry, it had just popped out of nowhere and he said – well you won't believe what *he* said!

He said, 'You know, I love being called Ape Face. It's a real neat nickname. Nobody in my class has a nickname as good as that.'

'You mean some of your friends call you that?'

'*All* my friends call me that,' he said proudly. 'See, the beginning of last year I told them that's what Annabel called me, and right away everybody did because . . .'

'Because they think Annabel is so terrific, right?'

'Yeah, right. But she won't call me it any more if she thinks I like it, so don't tell her, OK?'

'You got yourself a deal, Ape Face,' I said. Smart kid. Had me all figured out!

Eight

IT was two o'clock and I was just having a nice game of Crazy Eights with the Ape – actually, it's not the most interesting game in the world, but he picked it so what can you do? – when Daddy called.

'Oh good, I'm glad I caught you. I was afraid you'd already left,' he said.

'Left for where?' I asked, jamming the phone between my ear and my shoulder and shuffling the cards.

'Wasn't today the day you had the big thing at the school with Dilk and McGuirk and the psychologist to discuss our little underachiever?' Two-thirty with a box around it. And I thought it was a late lunch. What a lovely surprise!

'Thanks for reminding me. I better get going or I'll never make it, it's after two now, talk to you la . . .'

'Ellen, hang in there a minute. You haven't even heard what I called up about in the first place. Look, did you get the sitter and everything lined up for tonight? Because if you did, cancel it, the whole thing's changed. We'll have to see "Brucey and Betsy" some other night.'

'Aw, why? I've been looking forward to it all day.'

'I know, sweetheart, so've I, but Francie's Fortified Fish Fingers are in town and I had to invite them for dinner.'

'Say that again?' I said, stupidly. My mind was boggling.

'OK, we'll take it from the top very slowly,' he said. 'The client and his wife, Mr and Mrs Philip Frampton, she calls him Philsie and he calls her Francie, and you've heard me talk about them a thousand times, are in town and I invited them for dinner.'

'Here? You invited them *here*? You wouldn't! Not today! Invite them for tomorrow. Please Bill, how about tomorrow?' (Tomorrow — when maybe with a little luck, she'd be back.)

'No way, darling, they're only in town for one night. And they want to see the children so they're coming at six. I'll be home at five to change, did you do my shirts? And don't panic, you're one terrific cook.' Male chauvinist pig!

'You're one terrific surprise after another,' I snapped into the phone, but it was too late. He'd already hung up.

'Ape Face, where are you? Come here, quick!' He scrambled to his feet and trotted into the hall.

'What's the matter, Mommy?'

'What's the matter is I completely forgot a meeting I have at school, with Mr Dilk and Miss McGuirk and Dr Artunian about that adorable sister of yours, in exactly twenty-five minutes and I don't have anybody to leave you with, so put on your Mighty-Mac and let's get moving.'

'No,' said Ape Face.

'Who do you think you're talking to, Benny-boy? This is your mother, remember me? Now get that Mighty-Mac and move it!'

'No,' said Ape Face again. How do you like that? In my family there are not one but *two* male chauvinist pigs.

I took a deep breath, and in my most dripping-with-honey voice said, 'Would you like to tell Mommy why you don't want to go with her or must Mommy try to read your horrible little mind?'

'Because I have been waiting for Paul to come over and play all year and every time he's going to come either he gets sick or I get sick and now he's finally coming and I'm not going!' The kid's got more guts than I gave him credit for.

'Ape Face, I admire your spirit and I appreciate your problem, but I cannot leave two little six-year-old boys alone in an apartment.' He looked crushed. I felt sorry for him.

'Oh Ma, I hated Mrs Schmauss the most of all of us, but couldn't you of waited 'til Monday to fire her? Don't you know any other sitters? Someone who could get here fast? Someone who ...' Ai-yi, how could I be so stupid! The bluebird of happiness right in the building!

'Ape Face, I thought of someone. Quick, get the phone book.'

'Harris residets, Boris speakig.'

'This is Mrs Andrews, Boris. What have you got on for the next hour or so?'

'The sabe thig I had odd this bordig, Brs Adrews. Why?' Serves me right for being so grand.

'No, no, Boris, I mean what are you doing for the next hour or so? Are you busy?'

'Dot a bit. Would you like be to cub dowd ad play Dok Hockey?'

'Nok Hockey might be just the thing,' I said, with a thoughtful eye on the Ape. 'Come on down right now.'

'Who's coming?' asked Ape Face.

'Boris Harris, the most beautiful boy in the building. At least Annabel thinks so. She's in love with him.'

'Is he in love with her, too?'

'Not so's you'd notice,' I said. 'At least not yet. But anything we could do to help make Boris think more highly of Annabel we would certainly want to do, wouldn't you?'

'Sure,' said Ape Face. 'Like what?'

'I want you to let him think that your room is Annabel's room and Annabel's room is your room.'

'Why?' he asked in a tone of whispery horror.

'Because that's what he already thinks anyway. When he was here playing Nok Hockey with me this morning, he happened to notice what a mess her room was, so . . .'

'So you told him it was *my* room? Aw, Ma!' I was about to remind him that it was all for Annabel when the doorbell rang and Ape Face vanished into thin air. Embarrassed, I guess.

'Hya, Boris, how's the champ? I can't tell you how glad I am to see you. How do you feel about baby-sitting?'

'Oh,' he said, disappointed. 'I thought you wadded be to play Dok Hockey.'

'I do, I do,' I said, 'but not with me. With my son, Ben.' I explained all about the school meeting and

Paul coming over and how desperate I was and how much I needed him, and finally he said, 'Brs Adrews, you doh I'd do eddythig for you, but could I please see your kid before I say yes?'

'Ben, darling,' I called. 'Come out, come out wherever you are and meet Boris Harris!'

The door to Annabel's room flew open and out stalked Tarzan. 'Howdy, Boris,' boomed Tarzan. 'My mother calls me Ben but the guys at school call me Ape Face. Or just plain Ape. What do they call you in school?'

'Boris,' said Boris to Tarzan. To me, he said, 'I'll stay.' Then he blew his nose and much to my amazement, all his m's and n's came back. 'It's the oddest thing,' he said. 'I thought your Vitamin C fixed my cold, but upstairs in my apartment, the cold came right back, and down here it's gone again. Maybe I have a weirdo allergy to something.

'Oh well,' he continued in a businesslike voice, 'I know you're in a hurry so what are my instructions?'

'Just keep an eye on the boys, and answer the phone, and if you run out of things to do, you might whip up a smart dinner for four. My husband invited some clients home without any warning, and I just don't know *what* to *cook*.'

'Don't give it another thought. I'd be glad to rustle

up a little something for you. What time are your guests coming?'

'My mother was only kidding,' said Ape Face.

'Boris was only kidding, too, weren't you Boris,' I said.

'I wasn't kidding,' said Boris, sounding rather hurt. 'Mrs Andrews, I'm an excellent cook. In fact, if I weren't I'd probably starve to death because I'm the only one in our house who can boil water.'

'What about your mother?' I asked.

'Chinese, deli, or Chicken Delight – when she's in. Mostly she's out. When she's out, I cook.'

'Isn't that sort of a girly thing to do?' asked Tarzan.

'Look who's talking! The slob who sleeps with the canopy bed and the doll house,' retorted Boris. Ape Face opened his mouth to say something. I knew what he was going to say so I told him, 'Shut up, I don't want to hear another word.' Luckily he did what he was told.

'Never mind him anyway, Boris. He's just a male chauvinist pig.'

'I'll say,' agreed Boris, 'but he's going to help me chop onions anyway, aren'tcha, ole pig, ole pal.'

'Sure,' said Ape Face, who is not one to hold a grudge, and when I left, they were both heading for the kitchen.

Nine

THE Barden School, on 75th between Park and Lex, is, as the crow flies, directly across the park from us. Not being a crow, and not having the time to take two up and down buses and one crosstown bus, I took a cab and arrived just as everybody was leaving. Have you ever tried to fight upstream through three hundred and fifty kids getting out of school on a Friday? Talk about your lemmings! I was practically knocked down by three of my best friends, Ginger, Jo-Jo, and Bambi.

'Hey Ginger, hey Jo-Jo, hey Bambi, how's everything?'

'Just fine, thank you, Mrs Andrews.'

'Anything happen in school today?' I asked.

'Nothing much,' said Jo-Jo.

'How was English?'

'Fine,' they all said.

'How's Annabel doing? She doing fine, too?' They all exchanged looks.

'Oh sure,' said Jo-Jo. 'Mrs Andrews, please excuse us but we're in kind of a rush.'

'And it's not too safe, standing in the middle of the door like that on a Friday afternoon. You might get knocked down,' added Bambi.

'So we'll see you later, OK?' said Ginger.

Now ordinarily, I would have been extremely proud of my friends, because never rat to a parent no-matter-*what* is one of our first club rules. Today, though, I would have been grateful for one or two little scraps of gossip. About Annabel. About English. About McGuirk. About anything at all!

Funny about those kids, I thought to myself. They were in such a hurry to get going but they didn't seem to be going very far. In fact, they were standing still, halfway down the block, talking to each other and looking back towards me. Then, just as I was about to take the fatal plunge into the hallowed halls, Jo-Jo howled, 'Mrs Andrews, wait a sec; don't go in there yet! We gotta talk to you first.'

In precisely a sec, they were all three at my side, panting and sniffling and yanking at their tights.

'Well, what is it, girls? I'm terribly late for a conference.'

'That's what I thought,' said Bambi.

'That's what I was afraid of,' said Ginger.

'Who with?' asked my friend Jo-Jo, who never wastes a word in idle conversation. 'Because if it's the one with Dilk and McGuirk about Annabel . . .'

'*Mr* Dilk and *Miss* McGuirk,' corrected Ginger. (When I get back into my own bod, I'm gonna drum that prig right out of the club!)

'Oh shut up, Virginia! She knows who I'm talking about. Anyway, is that who your conference is with?'

'Dilk and McGuirk and Artunian,' I said. 'Why?'

'Artunian, too? Chee!' said Jo-Jo, wiping imaginary sweat off her brow and shaking it to the pavement.

'Listen, ladies, what do the words "I am already forty-five minutes late" mean to you? If you have something to say, I'd appreciate hearing it now.'

'OK,' sighed Jo-Jo. 'I'm not sure how much you're going to like this, but here it is: Annabel was not in school today.'

'Nonsense!' said I. 'She left the house at eight fifteen with her brother. And *he* was in school. How did he get there if she didn't bring him?'

'Take him,' corrected Ginger.

'Shut up, Virginia. Mrs Andrews, after she saw he was inside the front door, she waited for us around the corner. She said she didn't feel like going to school today on account of the English paper. She said she had better things to do and it was perfectly safe because the school never calls up to check on what's wrong with you the first day you're absent; they wait 'til the second day. She said she might see us this afternoon at the club meeting, all depending.'

'All depending on what?'

'She didn't say. All she said was not to tell anybody, and of course we never would've, but then when we realized you were here for a conference, we wanted to warn you ahead of time so you wouldn't ask them how Annabel did in school today, or something ghastly like that.'

'Ghastly is right,' I said grimly. 'When I get my mitts on that kid I'm gonna wring her neck!'

'Oh, Mrs Andrews, it's the wildest thing how you and Annabel look like each other when you get angry.'

'Shut up, Virginia!' I said and finally took the plunge inside the hallowed halls, which were by now deserted and gloomy and silent ... except for one lone typewriter in the waiting room of Mr Dilk's office. Behind the typewriter was the Secretary to the Principal, Mrs Betty Parsons. How or why the Mrs, I simply can't imagine. You'd have to be out of your skull to want to marry her. Old lemon-lips, old Brillo-hair, old twinkle-tongue. She feels the same way about me, by the way, and judging from the reception I was getting from her now, she doesn't like my mother either.

'Well, better late than never,' I said brightly. The response was zilch. She went right on typing.

'Yoo-hoo, hello, I'm finally here!' I said, putting my hands on her desk and leaning intimately into her darling face.

'I heard you the first time, Mrs Andrews.' She nodded her head towards Mr Dilk's closed door (typing all the while, mind you) and said, 'He has been waiting for you for over fifty minutes. Now, I fear, you will have to wait for him.'

'Fair enough,' I said and settled myself on one of those terrifically comfortable hard wood chairs, the kind with slats that get you right in the spine. Actually, I didn't mind waiting. There were a couple of things I wanted to figure out and this was as good a time as any to think about them. I folded my legs under me, Yoga style, rested my elbows on my knees and my head on my hands, which were over my ears to drown out the typewriter. And thought the following thoughts:

1) If I didn't go to school, where the heck did I go instead? Never having played hooky before, I had no idea where I might go. Maybe I went to a dirty movie

on 42nd Street where I am not ever allowed to go because it's dangerous. Could I have got raped or strangled by a depraved killer in the dirty movie? Or run over by a crosstown bus just as I came blinking out into the sunlight afterwards?

My God, my bod! I never thought of it before, but I'm not all that careful with myself. Suppose right now I am lying stone cold dead in the city morgue, and then tomorrow, let's say, my mother wants her own bod back, where does that leave me? Or to be more exact, *what* does that leave me? I'll tell you one thing, possession is nine tenths of the law and if anything like that happens, I'm staying right in here where I am, whether I like it or not. After all, she's responsible for this mess, she can jolly well go back to whoever *she's* been all day — Queen Elizabeth or Jackie Onassis or somebody.

On the other hand, if I go on being Mrs Andrews then I will have to explain to Daddy and Ape Face (who loves Annabel so much) and to all the teachers at Barden (who don't) how come I was careless enough to allow my little girl to play hooky from school and get crushed under a bus. Maybe it would be better to work out a trade with my mother and *I* could be Jackie Onassis.

Wait a minute! I've been assuming she was responsible, but what if she isn't? What if a third party switched us all around and it's not her fault at all? If that's the case, I can't very well refuse to give her back her bod if she wants it. Annabel, old sock, wherever you are, I certainly hope you're being careful with yourself! Don't even walk through the park.

2) I'm being much too pessimistic. What about last night's fight, when she said, 'We'll just see about that'? That's a threat if I ever heard one. Of *course* she's responsible. As a matter of fact, is there the tiniest chance that she really *is* in my body? If so, she's a better actress than I thought – all that marshmallow eating and stuff. And would she switch us around on the very day there's a big conference with the school about me? If so, she's stupider than I thought because she's putting me in a terrible spot. In other words, whatever I say about myself in the conference should depend on how long I'm going to go on being her. Which I don't know.

3) Maybe the best thing to do is sneak out right . . .
'. . . now, Mrs Andrews!' Mrs Parsons was shrieking, but with my hands over my ears I hadn't heard her.
'Beg pardon?'
'I said Mr Dilk will see you now, Mrs Andrews.'

Have you ever seen someone jump from the lotus position to a standing position in one move? Not in velvet pyjamas you haven't and you never will. It can't be done without falling down.

'Ups-a-daisy,' I said, dusting myself off, and entered the chamber of horrors.

Arnold Dilk is what we call a super straight. (You know: the short hair, the three-piece suit, the string tie – I wonder where you go to get one of those, these days? Brooks Bros, I guess. He says poim instead of pome, and not an *r* in a carload. Clearah, finah, brightah, et ceterah.) It was no small surprise, therefore, to find him leaning back in his chair, feet on desk, cigarette in hand, and smile on face.

'Come on in, Mrs Andrews; how've you been?'

'Well . . .' I started.

'Ah, you're not the only one. Everybody hates the hell out of February! But you *look grand*. Splendid! Have a seat while I get hold of Miss McGuirk and the good doctor.'

Out of habit, I headed for one of the hard browns, but Dilk, while he was mumbling instructions into the phone, hissed at me to take the comfortable chair. I did. He drummed his fingers on the desk and smiled a knowing smile at me while nodding his head up and down.

'Relax, Mrs Andrews. There's nothing to be alarmed about. We'll get this business about your daughter all straightened out in no time.

'Of course, I haven't had the pleasure of teaching Annabel this year, but I'll tell you one thing: That little gal is a personality in her own right. She has a real mind of her own.'

A fat lot you know about it, Silky Dilky!

'I guess that's true – most of the time,' I said.

'You bet it is. And we, at the Barden, encourage that kind of spunk and zip. We *like* to see spunk and zip!' (Spunk and Zip, Spunk and Zip, It sounded like a book about two Swedish brothers. *The Adventures of Spunk and Zip. Spunk and Zip in the Frozen Fiord. Spunk and Zip in the Sunken Ship.* See Spunk zip. Good Lord, was I going mad?)

'I'm sorry,' I said. 'You were saying?'

'... as long as it's accompanied by mature self-discipline and a sense of obligation to herself and her school.' Jekyll to Hyde in midsentence! The feet were now on the floor, the cigarette had been stamped out viciously in the ashtray, the hands were clasped together with tapping index fingers (this is the church and this is the steeple, open the doors and kill all the people) and the smile had vanished completely. When do we get the long nails and the fangs, I wondered.

'Ah, Felicia, Cassandra, come in, come in. Mrs Andrews, you know Miss McGuirk, of course, and this is our school psychologist, Dr Artunian.' Jekyll was back, a bundle of cheer, all of it directed towards the most beautiful creature I'd ever seen in my life. Not that I hadn't seen her before, you understand, but I thought she was a new kindergarten assistant – the kind that works for a year and then gets married.

'Well for heaven's sake! And here I'd been expecting the school ghoul,' I said, and immediately wished I hadn't.

'Sorry to disappoint you,' she said pleasantly.

'You're not, you're not!' I hastily assured her, 'I'm delighted to meet you, and how are *you*, Miss McGuirk?'

'All right, ladies, let's get down to business, shall we?' said Dilk, eyeing the wall clock. 'This meeting was a trifle late getting started, as you know,' he flashed me one of those now-you-see-it-now-you-don't smiles.

'Sorry about that.'

'– and we have a good deal to discuss. Felicia, perhaps you'll hand me Annabel's current report – I'd like to have a quick look-see before we all go over it together. As Annabel's homeroom teacher as well as her English teacher, Felicia – Miss McGuirk that is

– has a slight edge over the rest of us, wouldn't you say so, Felicia?'

'If *you* say so, Mr Dilk,' said McGuirk. 'At this point, I really don't know what to say. I'm at my wits' end, as it were. Here. See for yourself.' She passed the wretched thing over to Dilk.

'Yes. Let's see now. Winter report. Maths, 72. "Annabel has been having trouble mastering the techniques of long division. With more diligent application and attention to detail, however, we shall hope for a higher degree of accuracy in the future. Talks in class. H.M." That's Harvey Mills.'

'I know that,' I said. A pox on Harvey Mills.

'French, 68. "Although Annabel is developing a charming French accent, we would wish for more clarity in the written assignments. Her *Petit Cahier* is in deplorable condition and she cannot, or will not, comprehend the *plus-que-parfait*. Madame Murphy." You know Madame Murphy, don't you, Mrs Andrews?'

Boy, do I ever know Madame Murphy! To know her is to hate her. She's as American as I am with all the bad temper of a genuine French teacher.

'I understand she throws chalk,' I said.

'All French teachers throw chalk,' said Dr Artunian.

'Even if they're American?'

'Mrs Andrews, if Annabel had ever been seriously injured by flying chalk, I'm sure we would have heard about it from the school nurse. Do let's forge on, may we?

'Science. 80. "D.R."'

'Hey, that's quite a decent mark!' I said. 'What's the comment?'

'There isn't any. Donald Rosenman never gives a comment,' said Mr Dilk. There is no justice in this world.

'American History and Current Events, 65.' (Ook!)

' "Annabel can always be counted upon to make a lively and enthusiastic contribution to class discussion. Outspoken (sometimes to the point of belligerence) on such topics as our environment and the Women's Liberation Movement. She is occasionally inclined to be a touch intolerant of the other fellow's viewpoint. Nevertheless, she is to be commended for her passion!

' "Unfortunately, Annabel's interest in our country's past is not commensurate with her concern for its future . . ."' Mr Dilk looked up. 'I do enjoy Sophie Benson's reports. She puts things so nicely, don't you think?'

'Let's give her a big fat A,' I said sourly. 'I know, I know, that was uncalled for, and I apologize, but honestly, listening to you guys say rotten things about Annabel is not my idea of how to spend a fun Friday afternoon.'

McGuirk looked stunned. Dilk raised his eyebrows and sidled his eyes over to Artunian. Artunian looked cool as a cucumber, and in a matching voice said, 'Mrs Andrews, we can all imagine how upsetting this must be for you, but in order to gain meaningful insight into your daughter's present inadequacies, we must examine, as objectively as possible . . .' She's a living vocabulary list!

'OK, I said I was sorry. Let's keep going.'

'To continue where I left off,' said Mr Dilk, ' "past, blah, blah, blah, commensurate, blah, blah, future as is evidenced by the January text in which her confusion of the Annexation of Texas with the Louisiana Purchase resulted in a grade of zero on the essay question. If it weren't for this and several other errors of a similarly careless nature, Annabel could be one of the top students in my class. Regretfully, S.B."

'Have you any comments or questions, Mrs Andrews, before we go on?'

'Yes. What did she get in gym?'

'In *gym*? I hardly think that's . . .'

'Mr Dilk, you asked me if I had any questions. If it's all the same to you, what did she get in gym?'

'95.'

'Ah-*ha*!' I said, triumphant. 'Read *that* comment, please.'

As enthusiastically as a train conductor announcing the stops between New York and New Haven, Mr Dilk did so.

' "Annabel is a beautifully coordinated child, and a natural athlete. As far as team sports are concerned, her helpful and encouraging attitude towards less able playmates is a joy to behold. This year, her boundless energy has led her to investigate karate and wrestling, although I have repeatedly explained to her that the Barden does not permit coeducational contact sports at the present time, nor, in all probability, will it do so in the foreseeable future! W.H." '

Good old Bill Hauk!

'I'm glad to hear *some*body likes her,' I said, sitting a little taller in my chair.

'We *all* like her, Mrs Andrews, truly we do,' said McGuirk. (By the way, if you've wondered why I haven't given you any description of Miss McGuirk, it's because I swear to you there is nothing to describe. She isn't old and she isn't young – somewhere between thirty and fifty – she isn't fat and she isn't thin, she isn't tall and she isn't short, and so on. You get the picture.)

'All right, if you like her so much, what mark did you give her in English?' I folded my arms over my chest and waited. McGuirk looked a little uncomfortable.

'What mark did she give her in English, Mr Dilk?'

With an icy smile, Mr Dilk delivered the news. '37.'

'But that's *flunking*,' I said numbly.

'That's right,' said McGuirk, sadly.

'You can't *do* that to me,' I whispered. I felt a gentle hand on my arm, Nobody touches me when I'm angry, nobody! I pulled my arm away and the hand went back to Artunian's lap where it belonged,

'Mrs Andrews,' said Artunian softly, 'Miss McGuirk didn't do anything to you.'

'That's what you think,' I said.

'And she didn't do anything to Annabel, either. Annabel did it to herself.'

'But I've never heard of anybody getting a 37! 37? How could you come up with a number like that? What about classwork? Doesn't she talk up in class?'

'All the time,' said McGuirk.

'Well, doesn't that count for anything?'

'It counts for about 37,' said McGuirk. 'I tried every which way to give her a higher mark, but Mrs Andrews, how could I? She begged for an independent project. I *gave* her an independent project. That project was the rest of her term grade and she never handed it in. Today was the final deadline, and as you know, she was home sick. I don't even know what the project is.

'I could absolutely kill her! If she were stupid, I could forgive her. An ordinary, pedestrian, untalented, unimaginative, boring student, I could feel sorry for ... and as long as such a student handed in her assignments, regardless of how ordinary, pedestrian, untalented, unimaginative, and boring they were, I would manage, somehow, to give her a passing grade.

'But when a fine mind, with an IQ of a hundred and fifty-five, whose verbal aptitude scores are higher than a freshman in college – yes, Mrs Andrews, she scores *higher than the average college freshman!* – when a fine mind sits on its bottom – figuratively speaking, of course – and refuses to exert itself one little smidgen, well it's enough to make you SCREAM!'

'But I had simply no idea,' I stammered. 'I mean nobody told me any of that.'

'Well, we're telling you now,' said Artunian, the gentle moderator.

'So, Mrs Andrews, perhaps you understand a little better about the 37,' said Miss McGuirk.

'You know,' she went on in a quivering voice, 'one

takes great pride in being a good teacher. One does one's . . .

'I don't know why I'm using the impersonal pronoun,' she said, angrily interrupting herself. 'It's stuffy and archaic – and an academic pretension.'

(I am looking at Miss McGuirk through new eyes!)

'What I mean to say is *I* take great pride in being a good teacher and *I* do my best to infuse each pupil with a sense of self, to help him recognize and then develop his own potential, whatever that may be, and . . . and . . .

'Aah,' she said disgustedly, interrupting herself once again. 'That's a lot of garbage – straight out of teachers' college. What I'm trying to tell you, Mrs Andrews, is I admire and love your little girl. She is the kind of child every teacher prays to discover in her classroom; only once or twice in a whole career (which is just about how often a child like that shows up) would be enough – but when you finally . . . But when *I* finally discover that child and then I can't get through to her, or be of any use to her at all, then I have to face the fact that Annabel may be doing 37 in English, but *I* am the failure. And Annabel, in more capable, or perhaps inspired, hands than mine, will learn to implement the extraordinary gifts God gave her; but I have no gift, I guess, and I've botched the only real opportunity ever to come my way.'

And with that, she folded her hands and placed them carefully in her lap, opened her blue eyes very wide, and stared, quite deliberately, at nobody in the room. Every kid in the world knows *that* trick. It's to keep you from crying. It sometimes works and it sometimes doesn't, but it never works if you blink. She blinked.

'Oh, Miss McGuirk, *please* don't!' I was horrified.

'Here, Felicia,' said Mr Dilk, solicitously offering his handkerchief.

'Don't cry, please, Miss McGuirk. PLEASE!' I begged, in utter panic. But it was like monsoon season in the Ganges delta.

'Sh, sh, tears are the natural catharsis for natural grief,' soothed Artunian. Sappy skull-scraper!

'Oh come on, now. Crying because your dog died or your grandmother – that's sensible, but crying over some rotten kid who isn't even dead (as far as we know anyway), that's just a waste of good grief!'

'Charlie Brown,' added Mr Dilk.

'Hey, that's pretty good!' I said, admiringly.

'Yes it is,' said McGuirk, managing a faint smile.

'Rotten kid? *Rotten kid?*' repeated Artunian, 'Mrs Andrews, from what I have observed during the course of this interview, it would seem to me that in many instances, your behaviour is inappropriate and your attitudes bizarre.'

'Is that so?' I said. 'Name one.' Ladies unt chentle-men, ve haff here in our midst anuzza Zigmund Freud!

'Your visible discomfort at the sight of tears, for instance. To restrain yourself from crying is to deny yourself a perfectly legitimate and healthy emotional outlet. Children cry. Why shouldn't adults?'

'Children would rather *die* than cry!' I said through closed teeth.

'We won't argue about that now, however. Shall I go on?'

'Do,' said I.

'Aside from the fact that you were almost an hour late for this meeting, which, unless you can satisfac-torily explain it, would indicate a certain reluctance on your part to discuss your daughter's academic weaknesses, I find it revealing that when you finally did arrive, you demonstrated: one, marked hostility towards us for criticizing your daughter; and two, marked hostility towards your daughter for disap-pointing her teachers. Is it therefore possible that you harbour ambivalent and/or conflicting feelings about your child?'

'Absolutely possible,' I said. 'Doesn't everybody?'

'Are we talking about everybody's child in general, or Annabel in particular?'

'Listen, Dr Artunian, it's my turn to ask questions.

When I came in here and you three took pot shots at my daughter, my natural instinct was to defend her, right?'

'Right,' said Dilk and McGuirk.

'And, in no uncertain terms and with no attempt to spare my maternal feelings, I was made aware of the fact that she was an underachiever, bossy, lazy, irresponsible, and a hideous source of disappointment to Miss McGuirk here. Right?'

'Right,' said Artunian.

'So now that you have successfully convinced me that she is a rotten kid, not to mince words, and a stinker, you accuse me of being hostile towards her. Darn right I'm hostile! Why shouldn't I be?'

'Ladies, ladies!' said Dilk. 'This conference is degenerating into a free-for-all. Now let's calm down, shall we?'

He lit a cigarette and then said, 'Oh, I *am* sorry, that was pretty darn rude of me! Mrs Andrews, do you smoke?'

'Certainly not,' I said, and then remembered that only last week, in a homeroom rap session, Miss McGuirk had heard me give an impromptu speech on the dangers of smoking in which I cited my two-pack-a-day mother as a prime example of a person hell-bent on suicide.

'I mean, not any more,' I added.

'Oh, I was wondering,' she said. 'When did you stop?'

'I haven't had a cigarette all day,' I said truthfully – and pridefully.

'Well, that explains a great deal,' said Artunian. We were obviously friends again. 'You're probably suffering from nicotine withdrawal.'

'Gum?' asked Miss McGuirk, offering a stick. I took it gratefully, suddenly realizing that all I'd had to eat since breakfast was a few handfuls of cold macaroni.

'Ladies, could we please get back to business? In five minutes, the sun will be over the yardarm –' (Wha-at?) '– and I don't know about you, but I'd hate to miss the only reliable train to the Hamptons.

'Dr Artunian, why don't you speak for all of us? Will that be hunky-dory with you, Mrs Andrews?'

'As long as she promises to use short words and short sentences. No gobbledygook, just straight talk.'

'I'll do my best.'

'Terrific. OK, shoot.'

'Mrs Andrews, right up until this year, Annabel has been a model student, obviously a happy and well-adjusted little girl.

'But *this* year, we have all observed a marked change – for the worse. And what is the explanation for that change?

'Miss McGuirk feels she has failed Annabel as a teacher. Mr Dilk feels . . .' She gestured gracefully to Mr Dilk.

'That Annabel is totally lacking in mature self-discipline, and if she doesn't shape up fast, I'm going to kick her right out of the school, no matter how smart she is.'

'And you, Mrs Andrews, feel that she is, as you so pungently put it, a "rotten kid and a stinker".

'Now with all due respect to the three of you, I must admit that, as a psychologist, I find your reactions simplistic, to say the least.'

'What happened to the short words and the short sentences?'

'I think you are all reacting like simple-minded idiots, do you like that any better?!'

'Yes!' I snapped.

'I'm not sure,' said McGuirk.

'*I* am a simple-minded idiot?' asked Dilk.

'You *especially*,' said Artunian. 'As the principal of a school, you should know better. When a child undergoes a sudden and inexplicable personality change, it's either a brain tumour . . .'

'That's really grotesque!' I said, viewing her with distaste.

'And highly unlikely. Anyway, it's either a brain tumour or we have to consider outside factors. The home environment, for instance. The emergence of a heretofore suppressed sibling rivalry, for example.'

'Anh, anh, anh,' I warned, waggling my finger at her.

'She has a younger brother, Mrs Andrews. Is she jealous of him? Is there any reason why she *should* be jealous of him. Do you, by any chance, fall into the not uncommon Oedipal pattern of favouring your son over your daughter?'

'No, I do not!'

'I understand he is a charming little boy. You are sure there is no resentment of this fact on the part of your daughter?'

'Positive. Any other suggestions?'

Never in a million years would you believe the things that old bat dreamed up to ask me? Was I an attentive mother? Yes. Was I an overly demanding mother? No, not really. Had there been any change in the quality of my mothering lately? A fraction more impatient, perhaps, but with ample cause. The quantity, then, because if I would forgive her for mentioning it, the outfit I had on was a bit unusual, shall we say. Had I been out to lunch or was I on my way out to dinner? Neither one. I was trying it on to see if it still fitted from last year and was too busy to take it off again.

What about my husband? What about him? Were

there any problems in the marriage? *No!* My husband was not, for instance, domineering or overbearing in his attitude towards me or the children?

'Dr Artunian, you can ask me anything you want about myself or my daughter but it's none of your business how I get along with my father!'

'Oh, ho, *ho!* Mrs Andrews! Did you hear what you just said?'

'Yeah, I called him my father instead of my husband. So what? A slip of the tongue.'

'Rather revealing, don't you think?'

'No, I do not think! I have been here for an hour and a half, getting the once-over from you people, and if in all that time I only made one slip of the tongue, it's a bloody miracle. Look, everybody, I know you're only trying to help, and if I knew why Annabel's been acting this way, I'd be glad to tell you, but I don't think it has anything to do with her parents or her sibling or anything like that. Maybe she's just going through some stage or other. I'll bet that's all it is. So, Miss McGuirk,' I said, cheerfully patting her hand, 'on Monday morning I'm sure you're going to see a completely new Annabel.'

'Let's not get our hopes up too high,' said Artunian. 'We can't expect her to change overnight.'

'Stranger things have happened,' I said mysteriously.

'Well then, Mrs Andrews, I suppose this concludes our little meeting.' Mr Dilk stood up and shook my hand. 'And on Monday, we look forward to, if not a totally new Annabel, at least an older and wiser one.'

'You bet.'

'And you might tell her for me,' said Miss McGuirk, 'that if she will hand that paper in Monday, it's not too late to revise her grade.'

'I'll tell her the minute I see her,' I said, and truer words there never were! If I could only find her.

Ten

Do you ever get a premonition about something? Like you've lost your bus pass and all of a sudden you get an insane sixth sense that it's mixed up in your science notebook so you look and there it is? Well, on my way home in the cab, I suddenly realized . . . I literally *knew* by some miraculous sixth sense that Annabel was home ahead of me! I tell you, it was an enormous relief.

Unfortunately, it was also an enormous mistake. An utterly, totally, disgustingly false premonition, based, I suppose, on wishful thinking. If you think *that's* bad, wait'll you hear the rest: although Annabel was not there, her whole howling mob, fifteen of them, were. They had rearranged all the living room furniture to make a commando course for themselves and they were using a curtain rod for high jumping. The place looked terrific.

'What the bloody you-know-what do you think you're doing?' I screamed at them. 'Where do you think you are – Parris Island? Fort Dix? This is a living room. To be more exact, this is *my* living room into which my husband and Francie's Fortified Fish Fingers are coming in less than an hour. Now you get every blooming stick of furniture back where it was and pick up your Coke cans and your apple cores. I want your ugly little bodies outta here in five minutes, d'ya hear?!'

Boy did I scare them! It was like running a cartoon backward and faster.

'We're awfully sorry, Mrs Andrews,' said Jo-Jo, 'but when we saw you earlier, why didn't you tell us you didn't want the club to meet at your house?'

'Because I forgot it was supposed to meet at my house.'

'Well, that's not *our* fault,' said smarmy Virginia.

'SHUT UP, VIRGINIA,' said fourteen girls.

'And anyway,' I said, 'You should have better manners than to hold a club meeting in the home of a member who has vanished into thin air, even if the meeting *was* orginally scheduled to take place in that home.'

'Gee, that's right,' said Nina. 'You must be wildly upset.'

'And mad,' added Liz.

'That, too,' said Barbara.

'Oh, yes,' said Bambi. 'If I were her, I certainly wouldn't want to be her and come home and face you.'

'Maybe she's never coming home. You know the way she crosses against the light and . . .'

'Shut up, Virginia,' said Jo-Jo, giving her a poke.

'That's all right, Virginia, let's hear the rest of it.'

'I just mean the way she crosses against the light and rides her bike down Seventh Avenue and everything, well maybe she's – you know.'

'Dead,' I announced flatly.

'Oh, Mrs Andrews, that's a terrible thing to say. You mustn't let your imagination carry you away like that. Even if she *has* been hit by a car' (With her luck, it's a Number Seven bus), 'she's not necessarily dead. Maybe she's – she's only – uh –'

'Maimed and crippled for life?'

'Yes!' Virginia was relieved and delighted at the thought of Annabel's narrow escape from the great beyond.

Now I ask you: if you were my mother and you switched bodies with me and then got maimed and crippled for life by a bus, would you be content with your lot, or would you switch back to your old bod? That's what I think, too. After all, she may be a nice lady, but nobody's *that* self-sacrificing. Any moment now I could expect to find myself in some hospital, a total vegetable. I could just hear the club. 'Come on, guys, it's our day to visit Annabel the Artichoke.' 'Oh, again?' Groan, groan. Eventually, I suppose, they'd stop coming – even your best friends aren't going to cut college classes to visit a vegetable. In the long run, there was probably only one person I could count on. The Ape would come, bless his loyal and reliable little heart. Which reminded me, where *was* the Ape?

'Where's Ben?'

'Ben?' They all looked at each other stupidly.

'Yes, Ben. Ben, my son. Ben. The Ape.'

'We know who you mean, Mrs Andrews. We haven't seen him, that's all.' Steady now, Annabel. Get a firm grip.

'He was here when I left. I left him here with a baby-sitter. Boris, the boy from upstairs. If they weren't here, how did you get in?'

'Boris was here. Boris let us in. But we didn't see any Ape Face and he didn't mention him either. All he said was, "Is Annabel with you?" and we said we were friends of hers but no, she wasn't with us, and he said, "That's good." Then he said he was going back to the kitchen to finish cooking . . .' A few of the girls nudged each other and giggled. I gave them the hairy eyeball. 'Go on, Jo-Jo.'

'. . . to finish cooking. Which I guess he did, because a few minutes later he said good-bye, and left.'

By now, I knew the number by heart.

'Harris residets, Boris speak . . .'

'What have you done with my son?'

'Brs Adrews. I diddit do eddy . . .'

'You better get down here this minute and talk to me in my apartment where I can understand you!' Him and his neurotic adenoids!

'Right away, Brs Adrews, ad idsidetally, it's tibe to put the beat loaf id the oved.'

'Never mind that. Just get yourself down here fast.'

The girls were already climbing into their coats and heading for the door. I couldn't blame them — after all, who wants to hang around a crazy lady!

Boris got off the same elevator the girls got on. Without a hello, even, I dragged him into the living room and sat him down on the couch.

'Now listen,' I whispered, 'I'm not angry. I'm not excited. I'm perfectly calm as you can see. I just want to know, *where is he?*'

Boris was apparently in shock. With someone in shock, you shake them. I shook him.

'I was chopping onions and parsley,' he said.

'Go on.'

'And the doorbell rang.'

'Keep going.'

'So the Ape said, "I'll get it." '

'And?'

'And then I heard him talking to someone.'

'You didn't go out to see who the "someone" was?'

'My hands were all gooky.'

'Then what happened?'

'Then he yelled to me that he was going out and he'd be back in a while.'

'And you never even went to see who he was going out *with*?'

'Of course I went to see!' he said indignantly. 'Mrs Andrews, you must think I'm completely irresponsible! He was going out with a beautiful chick.'

'*Who* beautiful chick. *What* beautiful chick?'

'How would *I* know. I never saw her before!' He was getting quite agitated.

'You call that responsible? Letting a little boy be abducted out of the house with a total stranger he never saw before?'

'Mrs Andrews, that isn't what I said. I said *I* never saw her before. He obviously knew who she was. He also obviously was very glad to see her and when he left, it was willingly – he was not ABDUCTED.'

'All right, all right, all right, don't get so bubbled over. Shouting at me won't help.'

'Sorry,' he said meekly.

'Forget it. Now Boris, I want you to think very carefully. Did she say anything, anything at all, or did he say anything that might give me a clue as to her identity?'

'Let's see. She said thank you, young man, for taking care of him, she was going to buy him some ice cream, and I could run along now. That's positively all she said.'

'Before she came, or after she left, you didn't receive any strange phone calls? Were there any phone calls at all?'

'Only the mother of his friend, Paul, to say Paul had a hundred and one and couldn't come over. Ape Face was very disappointed about that, so I thought going out for ice cream with that beautiful chick – boy, did she turn me on – would cheer him up.'

By now, I was in what the movie mags call The Grip of Naked Terror. I always wondered what they meant when they said 'her heart was in her mouth' and 'her mind was in turmoil'. Well, in case you're interested, a mouthful of heart is something like a mouthful of captured frog, and a mind in turmoil simply means all the blood in your body rushes around in your head, leaving you icy cold from the neck down. As for 'butterflies in the stomach', there is no such thing. It's June bugs.

'Boris,' I said, speaking slowly and distinctly so I could hear myself over the roar, 'You are to be commended for your great taste in kidnappers. And now, if you will excuse me, I'm going into the bedroom. To make a phone call. To the police.'

That really shook him up. He followed me all the way down the hall babbling about how if anything happened to Ape Face on account of him, he would kill himself (not if I get there first), and couldn't he please keep me company — maybe he could be of some assistance (I told him he'd already been of enough assistance, too much in fact.), couldn't he help me call the police...

'Boris,' I said through the closed door, 'do me a big fat favour and shut up!'

'Can I say just one more thing?' he asked.

'If you make it quick,' I said, opening the door a crack.

'I love you,' he whispered.

'Your timing stinks!' I said. 'You should have told me that yesterday.'

'I didn't know you yesterday,' he protested.

'That's what you think,' I said, and slammed the door in his face. So much for my love life. Onward and upward with the police department.

Missing Persons, Missing Persons . . . persons . . . let your fingers do the walking (or the trembling), aha! here it is. What I wouldn't do for a push-button phone.

'Hello, Missing Persons? I am missing a person. In fact, I am missing two persons and maybe three.'

'Madame, we are a statistical bureau only. For missing persons, dial your local precinct.' I banged the phone down. Boris opened the door and poked his head in.

'I didn't mean to eavesdrop, but I heard you say you were missing two persons and maybe three. Who else besides Ape Face have you lost?'

'I've lost my mother and maybe my daughter. What's it to you?'

'Nothing, I guess. I mean, I wouldn't consider Annabel any great loss —' A headline flashed through my mind: INSANE MOTHER OF TWO STABS FOURTEEN-YEAR-OLD BABY-SITTER WITH BALL POINT PEN. '— and if your mother is anything like *my* mother, I wouldn't mind losing her either. But on the other hand, maybe you like your mother — some people do and anyway, I'm sorry I bothered you,' he said, hastily, and backed out the door.

OK, back to work with the trembling fingers. Local precinct, huh? Fine and dandy – as long as you know which one you are. I didn't. There were over twenty listed. What was I going to do, try them all? Rats!

Then I came across a listing called Know Your Police Department. I called it and the cop who answered told me the precinct for where I lived was number twenty. I thanked him and was about to hang up when he said, 'Wait a minute, lady. If you don't mind my asking, where'dja get this number?'

'In the phone book.'

Listed under what, he wanted to know. I told him.

'Gee, I didn't know that,' he said, very impressed.

I said I was missing two and maybe three persons, and I had to find them within fifteen minutes so I hoped he didn't think I was rude but I had to go now.

'Geez, that's tough,' he said, sympathetically. 'Have you tried Missing Persons?'

'Say, what else doesn't Know Your Police Department know?' I said. 'Missing Persons is only a statistical bureau.'

'Oh, I know that,' he said.

'Then why'd you ask?'

'I didn't want you to waste your time calling them.'

'That's very considerate of you. Are there any other numbers I shouldn't waste my time calling?'

'Oh, golly, yes! There's uh . . . lemme see, now . . .'

I hung up. *Unbelievable*!

'Twentieth Precinct, Patrolman Plonchik.' Annabel, you have finally lucked out, and it's about time!

'Officer Plonchik, do you by any chance happen to recall an incident that occurred at approximately twelve seventeen today on the corner of 71st and Central Park West, involving a darling little six-year-old boy whose mother was two minutes late meeting him at the school bus?'

'Yeah?' said Plonchik, by which he seemed to mean I should keep talking.

'Well, this is the mother speaking and I want to thank you very much for everything you did . . .'

'Tsawright,' said Plonchik.

'. . . and to ask for your help, because last time you only *thought* he was lost and he really wasn't, but this time he is definitely lost and I'm desperate!'

'Aw, come on, ma'am. On the level, now, you didn't just abandon him again and forget where? Try to retrace your steps. You already been to the liquor store. Maybe you left him at the cleaners? The drugstore?'

'Listen, that's enough of your dumb-dumb jokes. My son was kidnapped from our apartment while under the care of a reliable baby-sitter. As a matter of fact, the abductor was even *seen* by the baby-sitter. He says she was . . .'

'You mean *she* says *he* was . . .'

'No I do not mean that. I mean he says she was. *He* is the baby-sitter, a very reliable fourteen-year-old boy who lives upstairs, and *she* was apparently a beautiful chick who lured my son out for ice cream while *he* was making meatloaf in the kitchen and . . .' You know how people put their hands over the mouthpiece of the phone and think the person at the other end can't hear but they can? Plonchik made the same mistake. Rookie cop.

'Hey, Harve, listen in to this for a while, will ya? I can't figure out whether the dame is a fruitcake or for real.'

I decided I didn't have time to get mad.

'Shall I repeat the first part for Harve?' I inquired politely.

'That won't be necessary, ma'am, just keep going. So the fourteen-year-old boy baby-sitter was making meatloaf in the kitchen . . .' Harve snorted.

'And apparently a beautiful chick lured my son away while I was at a school meeting concerning my daughter. I haven't seen him since. And she's missing too . . .' There was another snort of laughter. 'Stop that, Harve, it's not funny. I'm not talking about the chick being missing, I'm talking about my daughter being missing.'

'See if you can trace this,' said Plonchik with his hand over the phone, 'I changed my mind. What we got here is either a nut or a child murderer.'

'Murderess,' said a new voice.

'Thanks for the grammar lesson. That you, Stan?'

'No, it's me,' said the voice.

'It's I,' said I.

'Who is I?' asked Plonchik.

'Who *am* I,' corrected the voice.

'Hey, goody, goody! We're going to play twenty questions,' said Harve, the joker.

'OK, gang, cool it. I'm in charge here, and what I want to know is, the voice that said, "It's me," *who is me?*'

'You is Officer Plonchik and I is – am – the upstairs baby-sitter.'

'Where are you now?' asked Plonchik suspiciously.

'Downstairs. Officer, I want to assure you that everything this lady says is absolutely true. I think you should listen to what she tells you instead of making fun of her and laughing and stuff. You ought to be ashamed.'

'OK, then,' said Plonchik, 'but make it snappy. I haven't got all day.'

'Neither have I,' said I. 'I've only got five minutes before my father comes home . . .'

'I thought your father had passed away,' said Boris.

'*Dead*,' said I. 'He is. I meant my husband. Anyway, here goes. Is everybody listening? I don't want to keep repeating things. Let's take a head check. Plonchik?'

'Here.'

'Harve?'

'Here.'

'Boris?'

'Here.'

'Stan?'

Silence.

'So where's Stan? I don't want to start without Stan.'

'Hey, Merve, tell Stan to pick up in the back, will ya?' I heard distant mumbling and then Plonchik got back on the phone.

'Stan can't come to the phone.'

'Why not?'

'He's not here. He's been out sick all day.'

'That's funny,' said Harve. 'I thought I heard him pick up before.'

'No, that was me,' said Boris.

'That was I,' said I.

'How could it have been you, ma'am? You been *on* the phone the whole time.'

'Forget it,' I said. 'Gimme Merve. I'll take Merve instead of Stan. You on there, Merve?'

'Yes, ma'am. I've been on since the beginning.'

'Aren't *you* the sneaky one! At least I don't have to go back over the first part. OK, I'll take it from the top, quickly.

'My son, you know about. My daughter — she started out for school this morning with my son, but after she dropped him off, she played hooky. I don't know where she went. For all I know, she's lying under a Number Seven bus.'

'Let's have a description of your daughter,' said Merve.

'She's thirteen, about five feet three inches tall, brown eyes, brown hair . . .'

'Long, stringy brown hair, and a mouth full of braces. Real ugly kid,' added Boris. Kill! Kill!

'But listen, guys, this is important. The point is I have also lost my mother.'

There were a few seconds of silence and then Plonchik said, 'I see. You have lost your son, your daughter, and your mother. Oksey-doksey. Let's have a description of your mother.'

'She's thirty-five, brown hair . . .'

'Wait a minute, *wait a minute*! She's *thirty*-five?

Your mother is thirty-five? So how old does that make you?'

All of a sudden, I was sick of the whole thing. Wearily, I said, 'Thirteen. I am only thirteen. I am just a little girl who has been turned into her mother. I mean I'm in my mother's body with *my* mind and I don't know if her mind is in my body or not because my body played hooky from school and hasn't been seen since early this morning. And maybe my mother isn't there anyway. She might have decided it would be more fun to be Jackie Onassis or Queen Elizabeth or who knows who she might want to turn into.'

'How about Helena Troy?' suggested Harve.

'Shut up, Harve. It's a fruitcake. Never fool with a fruitcake. You don't know what they'll do.'

'Gentlemen, please,' I pleaded. 'I'm not a fruitcake. I need your help.'

'I don't think we can help you, lady,' said Plonchik, sympathetically, 'but we'd be glad to find you somebody who can. Just tell us your name and where you live.' I heard a click.

'All right,' I said obediently. 'My name is Ann-a-aagh! Boris, what are you DOING? Gimme back that phone!'

'No way!' shouted Boris, slamming the phone down. 'You think I'm going to let them come and cart you off?! Mrs Andrews, are you out of your skull? You want to be locked up for life in a public funny farm? Some horrible home for nuts? If I hadn't hung up when I did, they would have traced that call – if you won't save yourself, some body's got to do it.'

Poor thing was all out of breath and almost in tears. I had plenty of breath, but I was almost in tears, too. He really did love me. What a pitiful waste.

'Darling Boris,' I said, 'I love you for trying to save me. As a matter of fact – and this is something I've been wanting to tell you for ages – I don't just love you for trying to save me . . . I love you period.'

'You do?' said Boris, in tones of reverence. 'That's more than I can say for my own mother, but actually, I don't think of you as a mother anyway.'

'No? What do you think of me as?'

'I think of you as a beautiful human being who still remembers how to communicate with kids. I mean, how many mothers do you know who'll sit down on the floor and play Nok Hockey with a fourteen-year-old. Answer me that!'

'None, I guess.'

'Darn right!' he said. He sighed. 'If you were twenty years younger, I could marry you when I grew up.'

'That'd make me older than you. How about twenty-two years younger.'

'Mrs Andrews, please don't start that again. I don't know why anyone wants to go back to their childhood —' he shuddered at the thought, 'but it simply can't be done.'

'Boris, you find it absolutely impossible to believe that I'm really Annabel, don't you?'

'Yes, I find it absolutely impossible to believe because it is absolutely impossible for such a thing to happen.' He gazed at me steadily with his solemn hazel eyes. The moment of truth was upon us.

'If such a thing can't happen, then I've got to be crazy, right? Just like the cops said. So why don't we call them back and let them come and get me?' I reached for the phone.

'Because I don't think you're dangerously crazy,' he said cautiously, removing the phone from my grasp. 'And maybe you're just having a brief spell, so let's wait another couple of minutes. Your daddy'll be home very soon now, and you can tell him all about it.' He was humouring me, and not very humorously, either.

'When my daddy comes home, he is not going to believe me any more than you do, and if you don't mind, I'd rather not be around when he finds out I've misplaced his two and only children. I'd rather have the police come and take me away first!'

The doorbell rang.

'Oh Lord, they traced the call,' moaned Boris.

'Hurray for New York's finest!' I shouted triumphantly and sprinted for the door. Before opening it, I peeked through the burglar hole to see if they had a straitjacket with them. No straitjacket. Just a plain-clothes detective and a matron. I guess for crazy ladies, they send a matron.

'Hello, hello, hello!' I said. 'You got here in record time. I didn't expect you quite so soon.'

'Well, we didn't have too far to come,' said the detective, modestly.

'And we would have called you to say when we were coming, in fact we tried to call you, but we had a little difficulty,' added Matron.

'Oh, I know, I know,' I murmured sympathetically. 'But that wasn't entirely my fault.' I allowed myself a quick smirk in the direction of Boris the phone grabber, the defender of maniacs.

'Is this the little boy we've heard so much about?' asked Matron. They certainly were handling me with kid gloves.

'This is the famous Boris Harris, the upstairs babysitter.'

'Aw, golly,' said the detective, 'we're mighty glad to meet you, but where are you keeping your own little sprouts, Mrs Andrews? I sure would hate for me and my wife to miss seeing them.' Aren't they foxy, those two! I bet they think I'm a *homicidal* maniac, not just a regular maniac, and now they're going to nose around the place looking for a couple of corpses.

'Well, I'm afraid they're just not here,' I said cheerily. 'I mean you're welcome to look for yourselves, but . . .'

'Oh, we wouldn't want to intrude,' said Matron.

'Golly, no,' insisted the detective.

'Say, you people aren't very businesslike, are you? I mean, you're not at all what I expected.'

'Shucks, hon, everybody meets us says the same thing. See, underneath it all, we're just plain home folks.'

'I'm certainly relieved to hear that,' said Boris with a comforting smile in my direction. 'Could you tell us something about the home, though. Like how big a home it is, and what the daily routine is, and is it easy to get to? Because I definitely would enjoy visiting as soon as possible.' Boris shot me another comforting smile. I shot *him* a smile that said, 'Why don't you shut up, Boris, because there is something very peculiar going on here and you are going to make it worse!'

Unfortunately, it's hard to communicate all of that in one little smile, even one little smile through gritted teeth.

'Young man, we would be tickled pink for you to pay us a visit. Any time you're down Gulfport way, you just drop right on in, hear?'

'Gulfport? Gulfport where?' asked Boris.

'Gulfport, Loosiana. We got a real nice little house – real homey-like. See, my wife and me, we may be millionaires now, but like I said before, underneath it all, we're just home folks.'

'Say, I guess I had you guys all wrong,' said Boris, delighted at this new turn of events. As for me, you would have been proud of me. I never missed a beat.

'Boris,' I said, 'Would you please entertain my husband's clients, Mr and Mrs Frampton, of Francie's Fortified Fish Finger fame, for a few minutes. Perhaps they'd like to see our kitchen on account of that's their speciality and all. Anyway, Boris, I'm going to ask you to be host because there's something I have to do in the bedroom.'

Slitting my throat was what I had in mind, actually, but I couldn't find a decent weapon. Not even a letter opener. Instead, I just sat on her bed and had a mad monologue with her. Or at her. (Whichever makes more sense.) At any rate, it was mad in both senses of the word because by now I was feeling good and mad but also good and crazy.

Listen, I quit! I've had enough of this. That's what you wanted, isn't it? You wanted to teach me a terrific lesson? OK, I learned a terrific lesson. But you better get back here fast because things are all messed up and I can't fix them. And if you don't get back here fast, *you* won't be able to fix them either. Daddy's going to lose the Fish Finger account, and he doesn't have any shirts, and the cleaning woman's been fired. Although I suppose it doesn't matter whether there's a cleaning woman or not because what's left for her to do? Answer me that? Ape Face is gone. GONE! Somebody came and stole him while you were out playing hooky or whatever you were doing. And Annabel's gone, too. Not that that's any great loss, but it's pretty hard to explain and if you think I'm going to be the one to explain it you've got another think coming, Ma. And when Daddy comes home any second now and finds out he's got no kids and a demented wife, he'll move straight to his club. (If he has a club. If not, he'll have to find one.) And then you want to know what's going to happen? I'm going right out that window. Splat on the pavement.

You better get back in this bod fast, or you might not have a bod to get back into! Never thought of *that*, did you? So if you know what's good for you, now's the time to show up. One, two, three, SHOW!

Where did that get me? Zilch. Maybe a slightly different approach:

All right, I won't go out the window. It's an ooky idea anyway. I'll just lie down on your bed here and close my eyes and count to ten, and you'll be back. OK, Ma? . . . nine, ten . . . Ma?

Oh Ma, please, please, where are you? Where did you go? I *need* you!

Ma?

MA?

MOMMY!

'Sh, sh, Annabel, darling. Not so much noise – they'll hear you all the way in the kitchen.'

Someone was sitting next to me on the bed. Stroking my hair. I was afraid to open my eyes and look, but it certainly sounded like her. I squirmed over to where the voice was coming from, put my arms around her middle and my head in her lap. A rhinestone button poked me in the cheek. Oh, wow!

'Sorry to cry all over your velvet pants suit,' I said.

'Don't worry about it. It's already covered with carpet fluff, and at some point or other I think you wiped your wet hands on it, so a few tears won't make much difference – the poor thing's seen better days.'

'So have I,' I sniffed. She laughed.

'Ma?' I asked, 'Did *you* do it?'

'Do what?' she said, all innocence.

'Did you turn me into you?'

'Yop,' she said, sounding quite pleased with herself.

'And did you turn you into me?' She nodded, smugly.

'It wasn't very responsible of you to play hooky like that,' I said, sternly. 'I was worried out of my skull. All I could think of was you might have gotten hit by a bus, and how was I going to explain . . .' A hideous thought suddenly came to me, triggered, I suppose, by the word explain.

'Ma!' I shrieked, clutching at her.

'What? What's the matter now?' she said, alarmed.

'Oh Ma, a horrible, horrible thing has happened. This afternoon, when I was out, somebody kidnapped Ape Face. I mean Ben. Somebody came and took him away and we'll probably never see him again. It's all my fault. I should be shot!'

'Is that so?' said Ma, calmly. 'I didn't know you cared.

'It just so happens I do,' I said. 'As a matter of fact, I care a whole lot. What's *your* problem all of a sudden? Don't you care? He's your kid!'

'Sure I care, but I'm not worried. Because I know something you don't know. *I* know where he is.' Cat and mouse time.

'Where? I demand to know where.'

'In the next room, playing with his Lego set. If you don't believe me, go see for yourself.'

'I believe you, I believe you! I'm just so glad he's back.' I wonder how he *got* back, though. Maybe the chick decided he wasn't worth the risk. In blue jeans and a Mighty-Mac he doesn't have much of a rich look. Oh well, who cares.

There was a faint tap-tapping on the door.

'Who is it?' said Ma.

'It's Boris,' said guess who? (Boris.)

'Don't let him in, Ma. He thinks you're crazy and he hates me. I don't want to see him.'

'Why does he hate you?' she whispered.

'Because I cut his head open with a shovel a few years ago.'

'I suppose you can't blame him for that,' she whispered, 'but why does he think I'm crazy? I hardly know him –'

'You spent practically all of today with him, remember?'

'Oh, that's right,' she hissed.

'He's in love with you, but he also thinks you're crazy.'

The tap-tapping turned into rap-rapping, and then pound-pounding.

'Mrs Andrews, are you all right in there?'

'Just fine, thank you, Boris.'

'Then why are you talking to yourself? Your daddy is going to be home soon and you don't want him to hear you doing that, do you?'

'What's he talking about?' she whispered at me.

'No, I don't,' she shouted at Boris.

'Never mind what he's talking about. I'll tell you later. Ask him what he's done with the Framptons.'

'The *Framptons*! Are they in town?'

'Not only are they in town, they're in our kitchen. At least they were. Ask Boris.'

'Boris, what've you done with the Framptons?'

'They left.' Uh-oh. 'They said they sure did enjoy seeing the kitchen and the children's rooms –' Ai-yi! '– don't worry, Mrs Andrews, Ape Face and I cleaned up his room this afternoon; we even washed the windows of the doll house . . .'

Ma started to snicker. 'Annabel, what kind of nonsense were you pulling on that poor boy?'

'Too complicated to explain, now, tell you later.'

'And,' continued Boris, 'they said since they'd

come primarily to see the children and the children weren't home, they'd come back tomorrow because they're staying over an extra day anyhow. Frankly, I think they just didn't like the looks of my beatloaf.'

'Beatloaf?' whispered Ma, wrinkling her nose.

'Naah, that's just the way he talks sometimes. Adenoids. Doesn't usually get them down here though. Oh well, he means meatloaf.'

'I'm sure it's extremely tasty, Boris,' said Ma tactfully.

'I did my best, Mrs Andrews. Under the circs, maybe my best wasn't good enough, but I did try. I guess I'll be going on upstairs now, though, because there doesn't seem to be anything much for me to do here . . .'

Pause, pause. Ma and I looked at each other and shrugged.

'He sounds so forlorn,' she said.

'I know, but what can you do?'

'Boris, dear, since you were kind enough to cook for us, I think the least we could do is invite you to dinner. Why don't you run along now and come back at seven. We'll all eat together.'

'Who all is we?' asked Boris.

'Mr Andrews and me and the children.'

I gave her a poke in the ribs. 'You goofed it, Ma,' I whispered.

'Mrs Andrews, are you *sure* you're feeling your-self again? I mean all that hysteria about the children being missing and the calls to the police . . .' Ma raised her eyebrows at me, and I nodded yes, '. . . and now you seem to have entirely forgotten about it.'

'I haven't forgotten, Boris, but I'm not unduly con-cerned about the children. And don't you be, either. Why, I'll bet when you come back at seven, they'll both be waiting for you.'

'One would be plenty,' muttered Boris. 'The younger one.'

'See?' I hissed. 'I told you he hated me.'

'You're going to find a big change in Annabel,' said Ma soothingly.

'I've heard *that* one before! Well, OK then, Mrs Andrews. I'll see you later.'

'Aw, nuts!' I said to myself, but by mistake it was out loud.

'You really like that boy, don't you?' said Ma.

'Fat lot of good it does me. You heard him just now, didn't you? You heard him!'

'But you apparently got along wonderfully with him today. And he evidently cares a great deal about you. You said so yourself.'

'Boris Harris cares a great deal about a thirty-five-year-old woman who is willing to play Nok Hockey on the floor with him.'

'Carpet fluff,' mused Mrs Sherlock Holmes.

'And besides,' I continued, 'so what if he likes my personality? He doesn't even know it's mine – he thinks it's yours. And he hates the way *I* look. If he said it once, he said it thirty times today. He thinks I'm ugly. He only gets turned on by beautiful chicks. Come to think of it, if he didn't have such a thing about beautiful chicks, I wouldn't have spent half the afternoon on the phone with the police.'

'Annabel, you're going too fast for me. Or else you're brighter than I am . . .' (You know, considering what Miss McGuirk says, I probably am. Poor dumb Mom! Darling but dumb.) '. . . so would you mind starting from the beginning, slowly?'

Anything to oblige. I had to start back in the dark ages of the morning because everything hinged on everything else. First of all, Mrs Schmauss was prejudiced. Did Ma know that? Ma admitted she did know that, but people were hard to get these days, so she'd tried to ignore it. That was embarrassing for Ma. Also, Mrs Schmauss refused to iron Daddy's shirts. Did Ma know that? Of course Ma knew that – Ma was the one who had to iron them. But Daddy was under the impression that it was Mrs Schmauss who ruined his shirts. Did Ma know that? Ma *did* know that Daddy didn't know who ironed his shirts, but she did *not* know he considered them ruined. That also was embarrassing for Ma. Did Ma know that Mrs Schmauss absolutely refused to clean Annabel's room? Yes, and who could blame her? That was embarrassing for me.

'Well, then,' I said, regaining my composure, 'did you know that Mrs Schmauss was secretly drinking our gin?'

'I was beginning to suspect her of that, but when you smoke, your sense of smell isn't as acute.'

'You didn't have one cigarette all day today and your sense of smell was better than a bloodhound's. Mrs Schmauss smelled like a brewery and at eleven-thirty this morning, you fired her. I hope you don't mind.'

'The only part I mind,' said Ma, 'is that I would have relished that moment myself.' I reminded her that it was her idea to switch us around, not mine. Didn't she think it was a touch greedy to expect all the fun at both ends? She conceded that point. Furthermore, she should be grateful to me for stopping smoking because if she could stop for eleven hours or so, she could consider the habit kicked. She was indeed grateful. Would I please continue with my story.

'Yes. Well, let's see now. When Daddy called up to tell me the Framptons were coming for dinner, he also happened to mention the school meeting at two-thirty. It was a good thing he called, because the date book only said two-thirty with a box around it and up until then I hadn't known what I was supposed to be doing at that hour.'

'Is that all I wrote down? Two-thirty? How *sloppy* of me,' said Ma.

'Maybe it was a psychological slip. Maybe you didn't want to remember.'

She cocked her finger at me and winked.

'You know, I'll bet you're right,' she said delightedly. 'Anyway, how *was* that meeting? Frankly, I've been dreading it for weeks.'

'It was a bloodbath.'

'Oh my,' she said, 'I'm glad I missed it.'

'Not as glad as I am,' said I.

'Anyway, to backtrack a little, with no Mrs Schmauss for a baby-sitter, I was all set to drag Ben over to the school with me, but he refused to come because he thought his friend Paul was already on his way over to play. I called up Boris, with whom I'd had a lovely time earlier in the day, and asked him to come down and baby-sit. He reluctantly agreed.

'He seemed like a thoroughly reliable person, and what's more, he offered to whip up some dinner for us, which came as a great relief, since as you know, I can't cook.

'So then, what do I find when I come home from that grotesque meeting but fifteen of my own thug friends dive-bombing around the living room, but nobody's seen me and nobody's seen Ben. And Boris has gone home.

'Extremely upset, I call Boris on the phone and tell him to come back down here and explain what happened to Ben, and would you believe he told me he let a total stranger take that little kid out for ice cream because she was such a beautiful chick he thought it would cheer him up? It never once occurred to him that the beautiful chick who turned him on could be a beautiful kidnapper! Dumb stupid fathead ox! End of story.'

'Very, very interesting,' said Ma, looking thoughtful.

There was another tap-tapping on the door. Ape Face poked his head into the room.

'Is it OK if I come in?' he asked.

'Sure,' I said. 'I'd given you up for dead.'

'Oh no,' he said. 'I was looking at a book in my room and then I fell asleep by mistake. Otherwise, I would've come in before because I wanted to give this to you.'

He held out the – helicopter?

'That's very nice of you, Ape Face. Thank you.'

'Annabel, how many times have I asked you not to . . .'

'Mom, it's all right. I *like* being called Ape Face. Don't you remember I told you that at lunch?'

'You did?' She looked over at me. I nodded.

'Sure, Ma. He loves it. You're the only one who doesn't like it. He loves it, don'tcha, ole Ape, ole pal?' I put my arms around his shoulder.

'Well, if you're positive it doesn't bother you,' she began. Ape Face ignored her altogether. He handed his creation to me again.

'I really want you to have it. I made it specially for you. It took me a whole week in shop.'

'Looks it,' I said.

'Can you guess what it is?' he asked anxiously.

'Guess?' I said, indignantly. 'I don't have to guess. It's perfectly clear what it is.'

'What?' said Ape Face breathlessly.

'A helicopter!' I said triumphantly.

'You guessed!' He was beside himself with excitement.

'You did a terrific job,' I said, patting him on the back, 'and I'm proud to own it. Thank you very, very much.'

'Oh, that's OK,' he said. 'Thank *you* for the ice cream.'

I heard him wrong, obviously.

'For the what?'

'For the ice cream. For taking me out. It was great. Thank you.'

I looked over at Ma. She had the faintest pleased smile on her lips. And she gave me the faintest small nod.

I think right then my whole brain went into the deep freeze. I could hear a clock ticking, but time slowed down. Stopped, for a second. Then, one by one, little green giant words began to defrost: *But if I took him out, then I am the . . .*

There were two more words to come, but they were frozen solid. Try again. *If I took him out, I am the . . .*

Annabel, you know what those words are. You're just afraid to think them.

Yes, because once you think a thought out loud – even if it's only out loud inside your own head – you can never take it back. That's not safe. That hurts. Because if the thought isn't true, it's already too late to pretend you don't want to be a beautiful chick. No!

Yes! Now say the whole sentence. Say it to her. She's waiting for you to say something anyway.

What if I'm wrong? She'll laugh.

Coward! Spineless! There's a full-length mirror

on the closet door. Look in that then. See for yourself.

My clothes are all new. Nice.

And?

My hair. Shorter, cleaner, and out of my eyes. Hair pretty, eyes pretty!

And?

Nose is the same.

And?

Mouth is . . .

Mouth is what? Different? Better? Beautiful? A beautiful mouth has a beautiful smile, a beautiful smile has beautiful teeth, and beautiful teeth don't have braces on them *anymore*, do they?! Smile, Annabel. When you say those words, SMILE!

'I am the beautiful chick!'

'Yes, my darling, you are indeed.'

'Why are Annabel's arms all over goosebumps, Mom?' Ape Face is right. I am shivering with cold, all of a sudden. But Ma's lap is warm, and a few more tears won't hurt the pants suit.

Eleven

IN our American history class when we've finished each chapter, Miss Benson makes up questions for us to 'think about' and then answer in essay form. The answers to the questions aren't always in the chapter, but they're related *to* the chapter, and unless you're a total retard, you can usually figure out what you're supposed to say. (For instance, if the question is 'How would you, as a British official, feel about the Boston Tea Party!' your essay might begin, 'If I were a British official, I'd be pretty tea'd off.' Then again you might not, because Miss Benson would give you a zero for being flip.)

Sometimes, though, you have to look the answers up in some other reference book, which is a bore – but Miss Benson (You remember her, she's the one who 'puts things so nicely', according to Dilk.) says, 'The purpose of these assignments, children, is to correlate the facts you have already committed to memory' (ha!) 'with newly acquired information in order to derive a deeper and more revelatory understanding of the material. Do I see a few blank faces? I believe I do. Well, then, I shall translate into your native tongue.' (smirk, smirk) 'The purpose of these assignments is to help you children "get it all together," as it were.' (Hey, Miss Benson, you forgot to translate 'as it were'!)

Actually, when you come right down to it, I don't object to the assignments – I just object to Miss Benson and American History. When you get to the end of a chapter, her system for getting it all together is as good as any other, I suppose. Which is why I am about to use it.

You see, we have finally come to the end, or almost the end, of *my* chapter. But in order to derive a deeper and more revelatory understanding of the material, there are several questions to be raised and several answers to be given. Such as:

We all know how I spent my day, but how, exactly, did Ma spend hers?

The first three hours – six to nine – were pretty tricky because Ma had to pretend to me and Ape Face and Daddy that she was Annabel. She said she found this rather unpleasant because she loathes marshmallows and if she can't have her coffee and a cigarette in the morning, she gets wildly cranky. On the other hand, being cranky made it slightly easier for her to snarl at Ape Face, which she felt she had to do if she was going to be completely convincing. She sure fooled me.

As soon as she'd dropped Ape Face off at school, she headed for the nearest drugstore and ordered coffee and buttered toast. The counterman said, 'Coffee might stunt your growth, little girl,' to which she said, quite truthfully, 'Oh, I always drink it at home.' To which he said, 'Oh, izzat so? I suppose you smoke home, too?' To which she also said yes and then realized she didn't have any cigarettes with her and when she tried to buy some, the counterman said it was illegal to sell them to her.

Anyway, when the stores opened at ten, she bopped from one to another for two solid hours buying sensational clothes for me. She had remembered to bring her charge plates with her, but she had to send almost everything home because, as one saleslady put it, 'We have no way of knowing whether or not your mommy would like you to purchase all these outfits.' Or as another saleslady put it, 'How do we know you're really your mommy's daughter? Maybe you're someone else.' (Ma and I had a good giggle over that one.) Luckily, one saleslady knew me and let Ma wear the clothes right out of the store. What *she* said was, 'Annabel, I'm sure your mother is going to approve of this dress. It's exactly the kind of thing she would have chosen herself.' (tee-hee.) 'And what would you like me to do with this – uh – garment or smock or – uh – whatever this is? I'm surprised your mother would let you out of the house in it.'

'Burn it,' said Ma.

After buying *The New York Times*, which she hadn't yet had a chance to read, Ma went to a little French restaurant she knew in the East Fifties.

'I ordered myself a nice lunch of Senegalese soup, tripe à la mode de Caen, tossed green salad, and more coffee, and read my *Times*. Or tried to read my *Times*. It was awfully hard to concentrate with half the restaurant whispering and snickering about me. Adults seem to be under the impression that children are deaf, dumb, blind, and utterly insensitive,' she said with disgust.

'Not *all* adults,' I said loyally. 'Anyway, go on.'

From two forty-five to four-thirty, she was at the orthodontist, having the braces taken off my teeth. The *wonderful* part about that you already know, but the funny part is that if she hadn't switched us around, I wouldn't have had the braces taken off to-day because I wouldn't have remembered the appointment. Dr Stein has an absolutely revolting personality and I forget as many appointments as I remember. When I asked her what she thought of Dr Stein, she said he was harmless enough (Not when he's twisting those wires he isn't!), but had an irritating habit of asking things like, 'Tell me, dear, how is Mother and how is baby brother?' when his hands were in her mouth and she couldn't possibly answer without biting him.

'Did you?' I asked.

'Only once,' she said. What a howl! What a kicky lady!

'You have to admit he did a lovely job, though. Have another look at yourself.' We both admired me in the bathroom mirror. (We were in the bathroom because Ma was getting changed for dinner before Daddy came home.)

'And now have a look at this,' she said, producing the plaster cast of my old teeth taken two years ago.

'Yick! Where did you get that?' I said, backing off in horror. I didn't even want to touch the thing.

'Dr Stein gave it to me. He wanted me to see how much you'd improved.'

'Gave it to which me? Me-Ma or me-Annabel? Because if its me-Annabel, I don't want it. It's revolting.'

'It's for me-the-mother, so I can see where all our

money went, and frankly, I don't want it either.' She dropped it in the wastebasket and the whole malocccluded mess broke in a million pieces, buck teeth and all. Zap!

Anyway, to continue ... After the dentist, Ma came home expecting to find me there (forgetting entirely that I might be at the school meeting), and when she found Ape Face in the highly capable (she was sure) but parsley-covered hands of Boris (whom she dimly remembered seeing with his mother ... terrible woman, his mother, and always borrowing equipment) she decided to cheer up Ape Face by taking him out for ice cream.

So far, the story checked out, but there was one thing I was curious about.

'Ma, I have a question: if the change in me was so terrific that Boris didn't recognize me, how come Ape Face did?'

'Oh, that was easy,' she said. 'When he heard the front door, he came running out of your room. I said to him, "Listen, Ape, if you broke anything of mine, I'll smash your Johnny Lightning cars," and he knew me right away. Wasn't that clever?'

'I couldn't have done it better myself,' I said in admiration.

When Ma brought Ape Face home after the ice cream, she heard voices in the kitchen. She also heard a grown-up yelling 'Mommy' in the bedroom, so she told Ape Face to play quietly in *his* room and went right into the bedroom, where she changed us back to ourselves again.

How did she do that?
I haven't the foggiest notion and she says she'll never tell me. Isn't that annoying!

What happened when Daddy came home?
I was in my room, straightening my tights and combing my hair when he arrived, but you could hear him all over the house anyway. He was howling about how he was late because he couldn't get off the phone – he'd tried to call for twenty solid minutes to warn us, but some idiot was on *our* phone. That was Annabel Idiot, chatting with Harve and Merve and Stan (No. Stan was out sick, remember?) and Plonchik and Company.

All right, then, where was a clean shirt? Ma explained about Mrs Schmauss and how she'd been too busy to iron one for him but not to worry because the Framptons weren't coming until the next night anyway and she'd iron one for him by then.

And then I made my entrance. If I could repeat the dialogue for you, I would, but there's nothing much to repeat. Daddy kept saying 'Hey!' over and over again. After about five minutes of that, he put out his arms and I got in them. I think he was very proud.

What happened when my grandmother called up?
Fooled you that time, didn't I? I'll bet you forgot all about my grandmother – the one with the house in Larchmont where they were going to spend the month of July while I was in camp? Well, she called up and my father answered the phone, and when he hung up he sat down opposite my mother in the living room and drummed his fingers on the coffee table.

'You've clearly gone mad,' he said.

'What's the matter?' she asked. I snuck into the room and joined my mother on the couch.

'This is February Fools' Day, right? Any minute now you're going to tell me it's all a joke, that your mother made it up, right?'

'Bill, what did my mother say?'

'She said that you said that you and I and Ben would be delighted to spend the month of July with her in the house in Larchmont while Annabel was at camp.' Ma looked definitely nervous.

'Oh Bill, I can't even remember the last time I talked to her ...'

'This morning,' I said.

'How would *you* know?' said Daddy.

'Because she talks to her mother every morning at nine, don't you, Ma?'

'I try. But that's beside the point. The point is, we always have so many things to talk about, it's hard to recall exactly what I said, but I'm sure I never said anything like that. I mean, why would I say a thing like that? I *know* how you hate Larchmont...'

'*I* never knew that!' I said. Ma glanced over at me, and suddenly she got the whole picture.

'Oh, Lord!' she said. 'I'm terribly sorry.'

'Too late for that now,' said Daddy.

'Gee, I guess we're all going to have a rotten summer,' I said.

'What's that supposed to mean?' asked Daddy.

'Well, you three are going to be stuck in Larchmont and I have to go to camp.'

'HAVE to go to camp!' Twin voices, both shouting. 'I thought you WANTED to go to camp. Nobody's MAKING you go,' said Ma.

'You mean I don't have to? Oh! I'm so relieved! Oh! What terrific news! Oh! I'm the happiest girl in the whole world! Thank you, thank you, both of you!' Oh! Am I one great actress! Although when you come right down to it, who wants to go to camp, an all-girl camp in Maine? Ook! I wonder why I ever thought I wanted to do that? I wonder where Boris spends the summer?

142

'Well, sweetie, of course you don't have to go if you don't want to,' said Daddy. He had the look of someone who'd just found nine hundred dollars lying in the street.

Is my grandmother going to be mad or disappointed or anything?
No. She doesn't like little children particularly and she didn't want them for the whole month anyway – only for the July Fourth weekend.

What happened when Boris arrived, which he did, right after the camp discussion?
But first, I have to ask you a question : Have you been waiting for this? Have you been waiting for the moment when the chestnut-haired, hazel-eyed, three inches taller, champion Nok Hockey player, maker of meatloaves Boris finds out that the metal-mouthed killer ghoul of Central Park *is* no longer? That in her place is Annabel the Beautiful? You *have* been waiting? Yeah, but not as long as I have. I've been waiting for three years.

Have you tried to imagine how it will all happen? After all, it could happen any number of ways. For instance :

1) When the doorbell rings, my parents are stand-

143

ing in the hall. I am standing shyly in the background.

My father says, 'Boris, come in, come in. I'm Bill Andrews; I believe you've already met my wife, Ellen?'

Boris steps forward, says good evening without a trace of adenoids. Smiles at my mother. Notices me; is clearly devastated by the sight. With super effort, drags his eyes back to my parents.

'Glad to meet you, sir. Good to see you again, Mrs Andrews.' The super effort fails. The eyes zoom back to shy Annabel.

'But who is . . . ?'

'Boris, surely you've met our daughter, Annabel?'

Boris faints.

Oh come on, now. That's gross! Boris wouldn't faint. Let's run it again.

'Boris, surely you've met our daughter Annabel?'

Boris marches manfully over to me. Shakes my hand.

'I wouldn't have recognized you.'

That's *dull*! Let's try something else altogether.

2) The doorbell rings. My parents are in the bedroom, and there's nobody else – oh yes, Ape Face. I could use Ape Face. Ape Face is in the hall and since I am on the phone talking to Robin (a boy called

Robin – English exchange student, senior in my school,) I say, in my lovely, musical voice, 'Ben, be a love, will you, and answer the door?'

He does, and I'm still on the phone so I put my hand over the mouthpiece and say,

'Boris, old bean, how terrific to see you again! I'll be off the phone in a sec.

'Ah, Robin, that sounds slick, but I can't tonight. No, really I can't. An old, old friend of mine ...' I wink at Boris. He realizes I am beautiful *and* a loyal, kind person – what more could anyone want?

I'm not going to bother finishing the conversation with Robin, (One of the good things about imagining: you get to cut out all the boring parts and go on with the juicy stuff.) I offer Boris a Coke. We're standing at the bar, smiling at each other and sipping Cokes when the phone rings again. It's Geoffrey. (Not Jeffrey, *Geoffrey*.) He has tickets for a sitar concert in Carnegie Hall for tomorrow. Would that be all right?? Sure, why not? Bye. Sitar. Sitar. Sitars in my eyes. My mind is wandering. Back to the telephone – which rings again. This time it's a black friend of mine called – let's see ... called – uh – Gordon. Gordon wants to know if I'm working at Head Start on Tuesday because he is ...

Now Boris knows I am beautiful, loyal, kind *and*

a liberal. And always on the telephone. But I haven't imagined a conversation between Boris and me yet. I think it's too late. I don't like this one . . . it's sort of out of control.

3) My parents are in their bedroom, Ape Face is in his bedroom, I am on my way to the kitchen to get out the ice – because now that I am beautiful, I am also a helpful, domestic (still Women's Lib, though) person.

In the kitchen, I hear a noise. I am frightened! Who could be in there, a burglar? Am I finally going to be robbed on this, the most splendid day of my life? Just as I am peeking into the kitchen to see the burglar, I hear a loud bang. I gasp out loud. But it is only the oven door banging shut.

In the kitchen, I see the chestnut-haired, hazel-eyed, three inches taller, champion Nok-Hockey player and maker of meatloaves, Boris.

'I was just checking odd the beatloaf.'

'How did you get in here, anyway? The doorbell didn't ring.'

'Subuddy left the door opid,' he said. He sniffed. In a minute, the m's and n's would be back.

'Hey!' he said, peering at me carefully. The great moment was happening.

'Hey!' he said again. 'Aren't you the . . .'

'Aren't I the what?' I asked, leaning against the fridge, playing it cool.

'Aren't you the kidnapper who snatched that kid out of here this afternoon? Yes, you are!' he said, holding a two-pronged fork at my throat.

'OK, girlie, I gotcha now. What did you do with that kid?' He gave me a gentle jab – just enough to remind me that the fork was still there, I suppose. Richard Widmark couldn't have done it better.

'Listen, you dumb fathead,' I said. 'That kid is my brother and I have a perfect right to do anything I want to with him.'

'*Now* what are you giving me?' he said with another jab at my throat.

'I'm giving you my name – which is Annabel Andrews.'

'Prove it!' he snarled.

'How?'

'Show me your teeth.' I did. He gave me another little jab.

'Nah, you're not Annabel Andrews. Now who are you and where's the kid, before I punch you full of holes?'

'Boris, leave her alone. It *is* my sister. She just looks different, that's all.' Ape Face to the rescue. Boris put the fork in the dishwasher. (What's the matter with him? My neck is clean. Enough.)

'I certainly wish you'd told me that this afternoon when you left with her,' said Boris. 'Your mother and I were terribly worried.' He stared at me in silence for a minute. Then another minute. It felt like a thousand minutes.

'She looks pretty, don't you think?' Oh, Ape Face! *You* are a loyal and kind person.

'Yes, she really does. You really do,' he said.

I smiled at him and said thank you.

He smiled at me and said you're welcome.

And that, folks, is how it really happened. Not very glamorous, but who cares. At least it happened.

How did Boris's meatloaf turn out?

I'm glad you asked. Right after the thank you-you're welcome conversation, Ape Face went off somewhere or other and Boris and I sat around the kitchen having a nice time talking about all kinds of things. Then the timer went off, and he said, 'Let's see how dinner is coming along. This stuff should be done by now.'

'I've never made it,' I admitted.

'Easy,' he said, cutting into it with a knife. 'It's

not quite done but almost,' he announced. To me, it looked positively raw.

'I don't like to argue with you, Boris, but it can't be. It's still bright red.'

'What colour did you have in mind?' he snapped. (Our first quarrel?)

'Meatloaf,' I said with authority, 'is supposed to be brown. Even *I* know that.'

'Meatloaf is supposed to be brown, but beetloaf is supposed to be red. This is beetloaf,' he said, with equal authority.

'Made out of *beets*? That's the most disgusting idea I ever heard in my life! It's to upchuck!'

'Listen, Princess, if you don't like it, you don't have to eat it.' He slammed the knife down on the counter. 'You know, you may *look* better than you did, but you don't *act* better. Where's the tin shovel? You got that hidden on you someplace?'

'I'm sorry,' I said meekly. 'It's just I never saw anything like it before.'

'Neither did I. But your mother was in a panic about those people coming for dinner so I said I'd slap something together. Then she went barrelling out of the house before I realized that there was nothing *in* the house to make dinner with. This is the best I could do.'

'What's in it?'

'Onion, hard-boiled egg, celery, tomato paste, basil, tarragon, tuna fish and Crunchy Granola. And beets. I just hope it's good.' He looked worried. Poor thing.

'I'm sure it's fantastically delicious,' I said, very gung ho. 'You've probably invented something. Beet-loaf by Boris. I wonder why I was so positive you'd said meatloaf.'

'I know why,' said Boris, wearily. 'It's because when a person with adenoids says, "Hello, by dabe is Boris add I've cub to make you a beet-loaf," you automatically translate that into "Hello, my name is Morris and I've come to make you a meatloaf."'

'Hey, you're absolutely right. Aren't you smart! That's a brilliant theory. As a matter of fact, I bet a lot of people think your name is really Morris!' Boris was standing with folded arms, staring at me, smiling the way you smile at an idiot, and nodding his head up and down.

'Yes, they do. Because it is.' ZONK!

How did Morris's beetloaf turn out?

Terrific, believe it or not. And my parents thought *he* was terrific and he told them *they* were terrific – in fact, he said he wished he had my mother for a mother because his father was dead and he didn't like his own mother at all.

'What's the matter with her?' asked Ape Face.

On his fingers, one by one, Morris began to list her faults.

'She's mean and selfish and she can't cook. All she cares about is buddy – she hates childred; id fact, she screabs at be all the tibe. If you wad to doh what I really thick, by buther is a crub!'

'Oh dear!' said Ma.

'Hmmn,' said Daddy.

'*What* did he say?' said Ape Face.

'Morris, did it ever occur to you that your adenoids are fine – you simply have an allergy to your mother?' said I, beating Dr Artunian at her own game.

Morris sniffed. 'That sounds logical, but so what? I still have to spend about nine months out of the year with her.'

'What about the other three?' I asked.

'In the summer, my mother goes to Europe, and I go to stay with my grandfather in Stamford. That I like. He has a big old house on the water, there's a sailboat, and a made-over barn he rents out. When he rents to families with kids, I play with them.'

'How big is that barn, would you say?' asked Daddy. (I don't have to go on with this, do I? The price was right, it was close enough to New York, it hadn't been rented yet, et cetera, et cetera, and sensational so forth.)

What happened after dinner?

After dinner, Morris and I played three games of Nok Hockey. He beat me two out of three – just the tactful amount, I think – and then he said he'd better be going home. My parents told him he was welcome to come back anytime, and he said how about tomorrow. We all said that would be swell. (Actually, my father said swell, my mother said lovely, and I said cool. Ape Face didn't say anything – he was already in bed.)

Then Daddy said to Ma, 'Hey, what about the movie? I forgot all about it. I was going to take you to dinner and a movie tonight. You still game?'

'Sure, I guess so,' said Ma, looking pleased. 'What'll we see?'

'I thought you said you wanted to go to that flick around the corner. "Brucey and Betsy".'

'I might have said that,' said Ma, 'but I've changed my mind. Let's see something else. Or we could all just sit around and watch the boob tube.'

'Not me,' I said. 'You guys go right ahead, but I have a long paper to write. Due Monday. I mean *over-due* Monday.'

Was the paper finished in time?

You betcha! I worked day and night all weekend and Morris typed it for me. It was a hundred and forty-five pages and Miss McGuirk gave me an 88, I would have preferred 98, but she said she had to take *something* off for lateness. Also, she said I shouldn't call it fact when its 'basic premise' was so utterly fantastic. Of course, that reaction didn't surprise me very much. After all, I predicted it, didn't I?

When did you do that?

Way back on page one, silly. You're not a very

careful reader. Don't you remember page one? The story begins :

You are not going to believe me, nobody in their right minds could possibly believe me, but it's true, really it is.

And the story ends the same way.

We hope you have enjoyed this book. There are more than 800 other Puffins to choose from, and some of them are described on the following pages

FATTYPUFFS AND THINIFERS

André Maurois

Edmund Double loved food and was plump, like his mother, while Terry his brother could hardly wait to leave the table and was consequently very thin, like his father. Nonetheless, they were all very fond of each other and the boys were amazed when, happening by chance to take a moving staircase to the Country Under the Earth, they found themselves split up and thrust headlong into the midst of the dispute between the warring nations of the Fattypuffs and the Thinifers.

The sparkle and easy humour of André Maurois's book is certain to fascinate children of all ages as long as Fattypuffs and Thinifers co-exist and remain mutually indispensable.

THE FURIOUS FLYCYCLE

Jan Wahl

Melvin Spitsnagle was pretty popular at school – his father owned an ice cream factory – but he wanted to be liked for himself alone, so one day he asked his father to give all the unsold ice cream to an orphanage instead of to his school friends.

Nobody much came to see Melvin after that, so Melvin said 'Pooh Pooh!' to everybody and decided to spend his time becoming a scientific mechanical wizard in the unused barn he used as his private workshop.

Then two things happened : his father gave him a beautiful Silver Zephyr bicycle and the great inventor Professor Mickimecki came to live in the town and these two events gave Melvin the brilliant idea of creating the *Generating Stabilizing Electro Carbon Condensating Atmospheric Pro-Cyclonic Compact Dynamic Magnet Box*, in other words something that would make his bicycle fly.

This very funny and original story is matched by equally funny illustrations by Fernando Krahn, and should be especially popular with boys.

For readers of eight and over.

MY FRIEND MR LEAKEY

J. B. S. Haldane

Mr Leakey was the only magician who could bring a sock to life, or bewitch a tie-pin and a diary so that he could never lose them. He wanted to run over to Java after lunch, and was going to use a touch of invisibility in the morning to cure a dog that was always biting people.

If you want to know more about Mr Leakey and his household jinn and the octopus who served his meals and the dragon (wearing asbestos boots) who grilled the fish, you must read this book to find out.

For readers of eight and over, especially boys.

THE MAGIC PUDDING

Norman Lindsay

This is a very funny book, about a very peculiar pudding. In spite of the word 'magic' in the title, there are no fairies or spells. Only a pudding.

Sometimes it was a rich odoriferous steak-and-kidney pudding, sometimes it was boiled jam roll or apple dumpling. All you had to do was whistle twice, turn the pudding round, and you could have whatever you wanted! Indeed the pudding was such a prize that there were 'professional puddin'-owners' and, alas, 'professional puddin' thieves'. One of the owners was Sam Sawnoff, whose feet were sitting down while his body was standing (he was a penguin), although Bill was just an ordinary small man with a large hat.

For ages eight to eighty, allowing for brief blind periods now and again in between.

If you have enjoyed reading this book and would like to know about others which we publish, why not join the Puffin Club? You will be sent the club magazine, *Puffin Post*, four times a year and a smart badge and membership book. You will also be able to enter all the competitions. For details of cost and an application form, send a stamped addressed envelope to:

The Puffin Club Dept A
Penguin Books Limited
Bath Road,
Harmondsworth
Middlesex

and if you live in Australia, please write to:

The Australian Puffin Club
Penguin Books Australia Limited
P.O. Box 257
Ringwood
Victoria 3134